修訂三版

超強英語力！

全真模擬＋精闢解析

聽說＋讀寫

全民英檢中級模擬試題

郭慧敏 編著

附 解析本
電子朗讀音檔

三民書局

 **作者序**

　　在 YouTube 上觀看 TESLA 創辦人 Elon Musk 的四大預測，包含全自動自駕車已成熟，無駕照也可以使用車輛、衛星互聯網即將問世、大腦可植入晶片以幫助治癒腦部相關疾病，太陽能成為綠能主流，才驚覺到我愛看的科幻片場景已經出現在真實人生。

　　不久前參加一場 NPDL 全球夥伴會議，會議中有來自十個國家約 500 人的線上會議，其中有兩次的隨機分組會議各別進行 20 分鐘討論分享，臺灣也有 22 所學校的老師參與。我發現其他國家的老師，多數為英語系國家，且都侃侃而談，相對地，臺灣的老師鮮少發言。此時的我當然要挺身而出，至少發言 2~3 分鐘，分享臺灣在疫情下的教育環境。

　　這兩件看似很平常的生活小事，我真心覺得臺灣很棒，一是晶片科技，二是防疫成功，但是在需要緊密的溝通與合作的全球化時代，擁有全球移動力的最關鍵籌碼就是語言能力的培養。談到語言力，想當然的就是從小培養，日日不間斷。那麼如何檢測自己的英語力？我想最直接的方法就是設定目標，參加英語文檢定。

　　撰寫這本書主要目的是要和大家分享，如何將努力學習的成果轉化在檢定的成績上。同時也期待每位讀者都能獲得實際的學習成果，確實提升英語實力。

郭慧敏

全民英檢中級簡介

新制全民英檢測驗是為了因應教育部 108 新課綱以 「核心素養」 精神為主軸，在測驗題型上做了一些調整，以符合現代人對英文的需求，內容更貼近日常生活，且納入更多元的圖表題、圖片選擇題、多文本題型等，達到整合資訊及活用英文的能力。因此，本書經分析財團法人語言訓練測驗中心所公告之內容，特別編製符合 2021 年官方最新題型的《全民英檢中級模擬試題（修訂三版）》，讓考生熟悉最新題型，做全方位的準備。

一、檢測程度

中級程度應在日常生活中，能使用簡易的英文溝通。

二、檢測對象

一般社會人士及各級學校學生。

三、測驗項目新舊制對照

聽力測驗

★第一部份：「看圖辨義」15 題 → 5 題

★第二部份：「問答」15 題 → 10 題

★第三部份：「簡短對話」15 題 → 10 題（新增圖表題）

　　→ 訓練整合圖表和訊息的能力，素養力 UP！

★第四部份：「簡短談話」10 題（新增此一大題型）

　　→ 談話內容取材於日常生活、學校、職場等多元情境。

★總題數 45 題 → 35 題

閱讀能力測驗

★第一部份：「詞彙與結構」15 題 →「詞彙」10 題

★第二部份：「段落填空」（調整選項為文意理解題）

★第三部份：「閱讀理解」（新增圖片選擇題和多文本題型）

　圖片選擇題 → 達到整合圖片和訊息的能力。

　多文本題型 → 培養整合多篇文章資訊的能力。

★總題數 40 題 → 35 題

寫作能力測驗和口說能力測驗的題型與題數不變。

※詳細資訊請至全民英檢官方網站查詢。

電子朗讀音檔下載

請先輸入網址或掃描 QR code 進入「三民・東大音檔網」
https://elearning.sanmin.com.tw/Voice/

若有音檔相關問題，歡迎**聯絡我們** ④
服務時間：週一-週五，08:00-17:30
臉書粉絲專頁：**Sanmin English - 三民英語編輯小組** ⑤

三民東大
外文組-
英文

① 輸入本書書名即可找到音檔。請再依提示下載音檔。

② 也可點擊「英文」進入英文專區查找音檔後下載。

③ 若無法順利下載音檔，可至「常見問題」查看相關問題。

④ 若有音檔相關問題，請點擊「聯絡我們」，將盡快為你處理。

⑤ 更多英文新知都在臉書粉絲專頁。

Contents 目錄

全民英檢模擬試題 中級 TEST 1

聽力測驗
第一部份　看圖辨義
第二部份　問答
第三部份　簡短對話
第四部份　簡短談話

閱讀能力測驗
第一部份　詞彙
第二部份　段落填空
第三部份　閱讀理解

寫作能力測驗
第一部份　中譯英
第二部份　英文作文

口說能力測驗
第一部份　朗讀短文
第二部份　回答問題
第三部份　看圖敘述

聽力測驗

本測驗分四部份，全為四選一之選擇題，共 35 題，作答時間約 30 分鐘。

第一部份：看圖辨義 🎧 Track 01

共 5 題，試題冊上有數幅圖畫，每一圖畫有 1～3 個描述該圖的題目，每題請聽音檔播出題目以及四個英語敘述之後，選出與所看到的圖畫最相符的答案，每題只播出一遍。

A. Question 1

Answer ❶ _____

B. Question 2

Answer ❷ _____

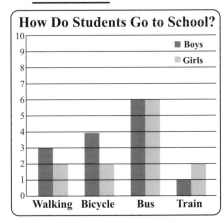

C. Questions 3 and 4

Answer ③ _____ ④ _____

D. Question 5

Answer ⑤ _____

第二部份：問答 🎧 Track 02

共 10 題，每題請聽音檔播出一英語問句或直述句之後，從試題冊上 A、B、C、D 四個回答或回應中，選出一個最適合者作答。每題只播出一遍。

⑥ _____
- A. Yes, I'm ready.
- B. No, I didn't.
- C. Yes, he told me.
- D. He quit his job yesterday.

⑦ _____
- A. I have his email address.
- B. You can phone me.
- C. In the cabinet next to your desk.
- D. It's about the new product.

⑧ _____
- A. The best thing is to take some rest.
- B. I would take medicine and drink more water.
- C. Your body hurts and you get a high fever.
- D. They are higher than you expected.

⑨ _____
- A. It couldn't be better.
- B. I'm glad to meet him.
- C. I have never been there.
- D. I have been to many countries.

⑩ _____
- A. I'm full, thanks.
- B. Thanks for helping me.
- C. We went to a new restaurant.
- D. I'm available next Friday.

⑪ _____
- A. It's not a big deal.
- B. I can handle it.
- C. Make a wish.
- D. You can say that again.

⑫ _____
- A. My boss is a mean person.
- B. What have you got to lose?
- C. Just fooled around with my friends.
- D. You can hire one more teenager.

⑬ _____
- A. I am. May I help you?
- B. He's from Australia.
- C. You can show me around later.
- D. I want to know the manager.

⑭ _____
- A. We'll stop by the hospital.
- B. It depends on the price.
- C. Here is your change.
- D. No, we pay in cash.

⓯ _____

A. He shouldn't have missed the important meeting.

B. I know. He didn't want to be noticed.

C. True. He wasn't afraid to speak his mind.

D. Right. He wouldn't stop talking silly jokes.

第三部份：簡短對話 🎧 Track 03

共 10 題，每題請聽音檔播出一段對話及一個相關的問題後，從試題冊上 A、B、C、D 四個選項中選出一個最適合者作答。每段對話及問題只播出一遍。

⓰ _____

A. Write a check for him.

B. Write a letter for him.

C. Fill in an application form.

D. Check his letter.

⓱ _____

A. Instant noodles are beneficial to people's health.

B. David won't stop eating instant noodles.

C. This is the first time for David to eat instant noodles.

D. The woman will be successful in convincing David to change his mind.

⓲ _____

A. They are friends.

B. They are colleagues.

C. They are neighbors.

D. They are classmates.

⓳ _____

A. She is going on vacation next Monday.

B. She finds a new job in Hong Kong.

C. She is going on a business trip the following week.

D. It is a shopping trip to Hong Kong.

⑳ _____

A. She has got really dark.

B. She is good at surfing now.

C. She likes indoor activities.

D. She has visited her family in the mountains.

㉑ _____

A. Her husband.

B. Her boss.

C. Nobody will go to the hospital.

D. She will go to the hospital by herself.

㉒ _____

A. She will hand in her report.

B. She will perform in the school talent show.

C. She will go to a dance class.

D. She will sing on the stage.

㉓ _____

A. Robert is Kevin's new roommate.

B. Kevin will have to pay for the repair.

C. Robert rented out his apartment to Kevin.

D. Kevin's refrigerator had been broken for a week.

㉔ _____

Fast Food Preferences

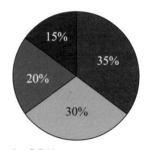

A. 35%.

B. 30%.

C. 20%.

D. 15%.

㉕ _____

Adult Pass $60

Child Pass $30

Senior Pass $45

Special Offers for Groups of 3:

*3 Adults $150

*2 Adults + 1 Child $130

*1 Adult + 2 Children $100

A. $100.

B. $120.

C. $130.

D. $150.

第四部份：簡短談話 🎧 Track 04

共 10 題，每題請聽音檔播出一段談話及一個相關的問題後，從試題冊上 A、B、C、D 四個選項中選出一個最適合者作答。每段談話及問題只播出一遍。

㉖ _____
A. A hospital.
B. A school.
C. A post office.
D. A museum.

㉗ _____
A. In a train station.
B. In a school.
C. In an amusement park.
D. In a supermarket.

㉘ _____
A. Why food will be free.
B. What time will the party start.
C. How people can barbecue.
D. What activities it provides.

㉙ _____
A. By ordering items online.
B. By buying clothes early.
C. By buying less than fifty items.
D. By making a bargain.

㉚ _____
A. On a plane.
B. At a train station.
C. At an airport.
D. At a playground.

㉛ _____
A. A library.
B. An animal hospital.
C. A zoo.
D. A pet shop.

㉜ _____
A. A frightened pet.
B. A chef baking a pumpkin pie.
C. A shop manager wearing a scary costume.
D. A shop decorated with Christmas trees.

㉝ _____
A. Stolen cars are often used in bank robberies.
B. The police were unable to catch anyone.
C. A bank was robbed this morning.
D. Violent crime has been increasing recently.

㉞ _____
A. A movie company.
B. A soap company.
C. An advertising company.
D. An Internet company.

35 _____

MENU	
Steak ··································	**$21**
Roast lamb ·························	**$31**
Fried chicken ····················	**$15**
Potato salad ·····················	**$11**

A. Steak.

B. Roast lamb.

C. Fried chicken.

D. Potato salad.

閱讀能力測驗

本測驗分三部份，全為四選一之選擇題，共 35 題，作答時間 45 分鐘。

第一部份：詞彙

共 10 題，每題含一個空格。請由試題冊上的四個選項中選出最適合題意的字或詞作答。

1 The local government is planning to build a new bridge in _____ for the coming tourist season.

A. corporation   B. determination

C. preparation   D. registration

2 The doctor _____ advised my father not to smoke for the sake of his health.

A. greedily   B. strongly   C. vigorously   D. amazingly

3 Wendy went to work, _____ her dog alone in the apartment.

A. leaving   B. she leaving   C. she was left   D. being left

4 There are many _____ on the road to success, but we should never give up.

A. ornaments   B. obstacles   C. beverages   D. souvenirs

5 On the street _____ crying for his mother.

A. a little boy is   B. is a little boy

C. a little boy who   D. where a little boy

6 The clock on the wall _____. Maybe we should change the batteries.

A. worked out   B. took over   C. shook off   D. ran down

7 Denny was able to _____ difficulties and won a scholarship.

A. overcome   B. present   C. declare   D. provide

8 Sometimes parents have problems _____ with their children due to the generation gap.

A. communicate   B. communicated

C. communicating   D. to communicate

9 After a _____ period of investigation, the judge found the suspect innocent and set him free at last.

A. prolonged   B. confined   C. fascinating   D. satisfying

⑩ The ball game was supposed to start at 9 a.m., but it was _____ because of a shower of rain.

   A. postponed   B. substituted   C. twisted   D. appeared

第二部份：段落填空

共 10 題，包括二個段落，每個段落各含 5 個空格。請由試題冊上四個選項中選出最適合題意的字或詞作答。

Questions 11–15

You may have some knowledge that you can share with others. In that case, you can create an E-book. The most important part is to have a topic that is ___(11)___ and spread your knowledge. Once you have ___(12)___, you can give a summary of your idea or a writing plan to guide you when you are writing E-books.

It is said that E-books are the future of ___(13)___. With your original idea and a lot of ___(14)___, you can provide others the opportunity to download your E-books. You can even start your own business by selling E-books. Maybe you will make a fortune than you ___(15)___ by this.

⑪ A. in return   B. in demand   C. in detail   D. in vain

⑫ A. come up with a specific idea

   B. got along with your classmates

   C. fed up with your household chores

   D. fallen in love with someone

⑬ A. career   B. family   C. publishing   D. friendship

⑭ A. distribution   B. prescription   C. nomination   D. ambition

⑮ A. imagined   B. emerged   C. managed   D. maintained

Questions 16–20

National Geographic Channel (NGC) has an interesting program called *Invasion Earth*. The show tries to find out if we are really alone in the universe. It starts by explaining that people have questioned whether there is intelligent life in outer space ever since humans ___(16)___ into the sky. Then, a collection of many sightings of unidentified flying objects is presented to the audience. Some of the sightings are in documentary format. Others are showing actual footage and ___(17)___ in-depth interviews with witnesses. In fact, people may find it ___(18)___ that some of the cases can't be explained by science. They are ___(19)___. However, not all of the sources are reliable because some witnesses interviewed in the program look as if they are crazy or drug abusers. That's why some people regard these sightings ___(20)___ mischief.

_____ ⑯ A. was gazed   B. to gaze   C. are gazing   D. gazed

_____ ⑰ A. combined with   B. relied on

        C. benefited from   D. closed up

_____ ⑱ A. uncomfortable   B. unsuitable

        C. unbelievable   D. reasonable

_____ ⑲ A. neither military drills nor natural phenomenon

        B. not only foolish, but also ridiculous

        C. either schoolwork or a job interview

        D. both delicious and pleasant

_____ ⑳ A. in   B. as   C. of   D. from

第三部份：閱讀理解

共 15 題，包括數篇短文，每篇短文後有 2~4 個相關問題。請由試題冊上四個選項中選出最適合者作答。

Questions 21–23　are based on information provided in the following online chat and menu.

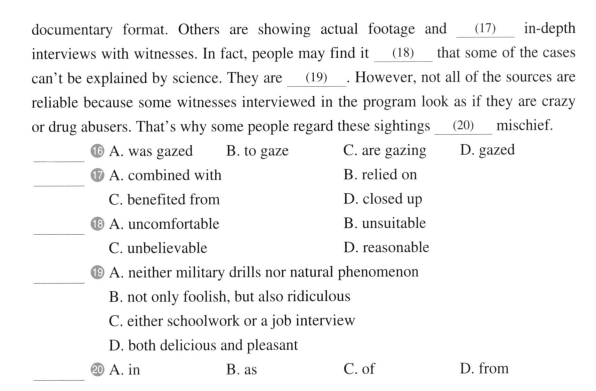

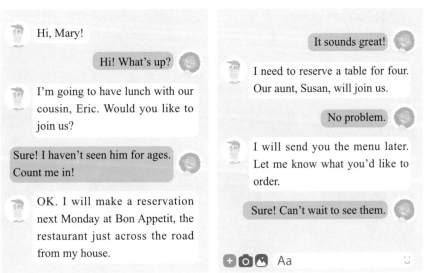

_____ ㉑ What is the purpose of the online chat?

A. To introduce Mary to Eric.

B. To order food and drinks.

C. To invite Mary for lunch.

D. To make a table reservation.

_____ ㉒ What is true about Mary and Eric's relationship?

A. They are cousins.

B. Mary is Eric's aunt.

C. They are long-time friends.

D. Eric is an acquaintance of Mary's.

_____ ㉓ If Mary wants to have snack, which of the following will most likely be ordered?

A.   B.   C.   D.

Questions 24–25

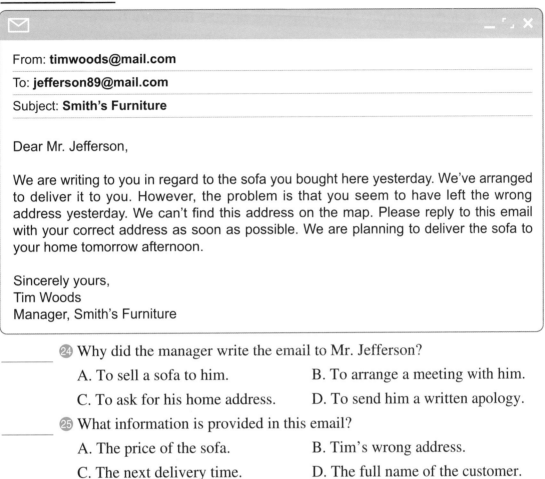

From: **timwoods@mail.com**

To: **jefferson89@mail.com**

Subject: **Smith's Furniture**

Dear Mr. Jefferson,

We are writing to you in regard to the sofa you bought here yesterday. We've arranged to deliver it to you. However, the problem is that you seem to have left the wrong address yesterday. We can't find this address on the map. Please reply to this email with your correct address as soon as possible. We are planning to deliver the sofa to your home tomorrow afternoon.

Sincerely yours,
Tim Woods
Manager, Smith's Furniture

㉔ Why did the manager write the email to Mr. Jefferson?

A. To sell a sofa to him.   B. To arrange a meeting with him.

C. To ask for his home address.   D. To send him a written apology.

㉕ What information is provided in this email?

A. The price of the sofa.   B. Tim's wrong address.

C. The next delivery time.   D. The full name of the customer.

Questions 26–29

It was with reason that *Forbes* magazine listed Tory Burch as one of the world's most powerful women. In just ten years, she has built a successful fashion empire. In the process, she has also <u>amassed</u> a net worth of over a billion dollars.

It may surprise some people that Burch has no formal design training. Before starting her own fashion label, she had gained a great deal of experience while working in the fashion industry. After graduating from university with an art history major, she moved to New York and got her first job there. It was here that she developed her love of fashion and skills in marketing and public relations. She worked with some of the world's most famous and creative designers, including Vera Wang and Ralph Lauren.

The Tory Burch fashion label was established in 2004, and its logo was made up of two Ts in a circle. It was also at this time that the first Tory Burch store opened. Now, there are so many Tory Burch stores located everywhere around the world. Besides being a successful entrepreneur, Tory Burch is also a warm-hearted person. She set up a foundation to provide affordable loans and business education for women who wish to be successful entrepreneurs.

_____ 26 Which of the following is **NOT** true about Tory Burch?

    A. She is a billionaire.

    B. She has a degree in fashion and design.

    C. She has built a successful fashion empire.

    D. She is considered one of the world's most influential women.

_____ 27 What is the purpose of this article?

    A. To share the secret of Tory Burch's success.

    B. To pay tribute to fashion designers.

    C. To introduce a fashion label.

    D. To explain how to open new branches around the world.

_____ 28 The word "amassed" in first paragraph is closest in meaning to _____ .

    A. lost   B. spent   C. inherited   D. accumulated

_____ 29 What can be inferred from this article?

    A. Tory Burch is a native New Yorker.

    B. Tory Burch founds a charitable organization.

    C. People can only buy Tory Burch's products in Shanghai.

    D. *Forbes* magazine chooses Tory Burch as one of the most powerful women in the world at random.

Questions 30–32

What are dog owners supposed to do with their dogs when they are at work? Staying home alone for their dogs is outdated. Now, the owners can choose to send their dogs to the dog day care and training center instead of leaving them at home.

The center is managed by highly experienced experts and professional dog trainers. Dogs will be cared for in a pleasant environment in the center. Studies have shown that dogs can benefit from day care, especially those dogs that are suffering from anxiety when left alone. The center provides a variety of services to dogs in order to make dogs feel safe and comfortable. Maybe you can consider the possibility of sending your dog to the center when you are busy.

⓿ Which of the following statements is true?

    A. There are many experienced experts in the center.

    B. The center is suitable for dog keepers who are rich.

    C. All of the dogs are anxious when they are alone.

    D. The center creates a pleasant environment for kids.

㉛ What does the writer suggest in the passage?

    A. Dogs tend to have stomach disorder when being alone.

    B. Dogs' anxiety will be improved in the center.

    C. The center is managed by amateurs.

    D. The center will teach dogs math like a school for kids.

㉜ Who is **NOT** mentioned in the passage?

    A. Experts.   B. Trainers.   C. Dog keepers.   D. Shopkeepers.

Questions 33–35

    Close-up magic and stage magic are the two common forms of magic. Close-up magic is usually performed very close to a small audience. The magician uses simple everyday props such as cards, coins, or a handkerchief to perform impressive tricks. On the other hand, stage magic is usually performed on a stage in front of a large audience. It will often involve the use of large and complex props. Moreover, mentalism is a magic that magicians performing tricks like they are able to read someone's mind.

    Street magic is a type of magic that magicians can use every style of magic to perform. However, guerrilla magic, which is a modern style of street magic, has become popular recently. David Blaine, an American illusionist, is credited with starting this latest development in magic. He would perform a trick in a public place. For example, he would go up to couples in the street and borrow a ten-dollar bill from them. Then, he tore the bill into pieces and put them in his mouth. After a few seconds, he could pull an undamaged bill out of his mouth. Isn't it amazing? He even had his own TV show!

_____ ㉝ Which type of magic creates the illusion of being able to read a person's thoughts?

A. Close-up magic.
B. Stage magic.
C. Mentalism.
D. Guerrilla magic.

_____ ㉞ What is the article mainly about?

A. Talented magicians in the world.
B. A brief introduction to magic.
C. How to become a magician.
D. An entertaining TV show.

_____ ㉟ Which of the following statements is true about stage magic?

A. Its props are more complicated than others.
B. It is performed when the audience is near the magician.
C. It has become more and more popular recently.
D. It has become a hit because of David Blaine.

寫作能力測驗

第一部份：中譯英

說明：請將下列的一段中文翻譯成通順、達意且前後連貫的英文。

　　很久以前，邪惡的精靈會前來攻擊過生日的那個人。邪惡的精靈帶給人們恐懼，所以家人朋友會環繞在過生日的人的四周。他們發出噪音以趕走精靈。同時也獻上他們的祝福。

_____

_____

_____

_____

第二部份：英文作文

說明：請依下面所提供的文字提示寫一篇英文作文，長度約120字（8至12個句子）。作文可以是一個完整的段落，也可以分段。（評分重點包括內容、組織、文法、用字遣詞、標點符號、大小寫。）

提示：最近很多人開始騎腳踏車上下班或作為休閒活動。你認為全球腳踏車日益普遍的原因何在？請說明你的看法。

_____

_____

_____

_____

_____

_____

_____

_____

_____

_____

口說能力測驗

🎧 Track 05

請在 15 秒內完成並唸出下列自我介紹的句子：
My seat number is (座位號碼後 5 碼), and my registration number is (考試號碼後 5 碼).

第一部份：朗讀短文

請先利用一分鐘的時間閱讀下面的短文,然後在二分鐘內以正常的速度,清楚正確的讀出下面的短文,閱讀時請不要發出聲音。

Honesty is the key point of a child's character. It is hard for young child to tell the difference between reality and fantasy, and therefore between what is true and what is false.

*　　　　　*　　　　　*

Scientists had found that learning and memory have a lot to do with sleep. Five students were subjects in Walker's research, and in the research, they were kept awake for more than 24 hours before being tested on their ability to memorize lists of words. The result showed a decrease of 40% in their ability. In the research, he has also made significant discoveries about the things happening when we get enough sleep.

第二部份：回答問題 🎧 Track 06

共十題。題目已事先錄音,每題經由耳機播出二次,不印在試卷上。第一至五題,每題回答時間 15 秒;第六至十題,每題回答時間 30 秒。每題播出後,請立即回答。回答時,不一定要用完整的句子,但請在作答時間內盡量的表達。

下面有一張圖片及四個相關的問題，請在一分半鐘內完成作答。作答時，請直接回答，不需將題號及題目唸出。

首先請利用 30 秒的時間看圖及問題。

1. 照片裡發生什麼事？
2. 照片裡的人是誰？
3. 照片中建築物的狀況如何？
4. 如果尚有時間，請詳細描述圖片中的景物。

請將下列自我介紹的句子再唸一遍：

My seat number is (<u>座位號碼後 5 碼</u>), and my registration number is (<u>考試號碼後 5 碼</u>).

全民英檢 模擬試題 中級 TEST 2

聽力測驗
第一部份　看圖辨義
第二部份　問答
第三部份　簡短對話
第四部份　簡短談話

閱讀能力測驗
第一部份　詞彙
第二部份　段落填空
第三部份　閱讀理解

寫作能力測驗
第一部份　中譯英
第二部份　英文作文

口說能力測驗
第一部份　朗讀短文
第二部份　回答問題
第三部份　看圖敘述

聽力測驗

本測驗分四部份，全為四選一之選擇題，共 35 題，作答時間約 30 分鐘。

第一部份：看圖辨義 🎧 Track 08

共 5 題，試題冊上有數幅圖畫，每一圖畫有 1～3 個描述該圖的題目，每題請聽音檔播出題目以及四個英語敘述之後，選出與所看到的圖畫最相符的答案，每題只播出一遍。

A. Questions 1 and 2

Answer ❶ _____ ❷ _____

B. Question 3

Answer ❸ _____

C. Question 4

Answer 4 _____

D. Question 5

Answer 5 _____

第二部份：問答 🎧 Track 09

共 10 題，每題請聽音檔播出一英語問句或直述句之後，從試題冊上 A、B、C、D 四個回答或回應中，選出一個最適合者作答。每題只播出一遍。

⑥ _____
A. Please wait. I'll refill it with orange juice later.
B. What were his bad dreams about?
C. Congratulations! We are so proud of you.
D. It must have required a great deal of determination.

⑦ _____
A. It's fine.
B. Tea, please.
C. Well-done.
D. It smells good.

⑧ _____
A. Run as fast as you can.
B. You are not sorry at all!
C. Sure. Call me on my cellphone, OK?
D. Don't let me hear you talking like that again.

⑨ _____
A. See you around.
B. I have heard so much about you.
C. What's the matter with you?
D. You guessed right.

⑩ _____
A. Why don't you come with me?
B. Mind your own business.
C. It made no sense.
D. You should take a rest.

⑪ _____
A. See you tomorrow.
B. The weather is nice today.
C. How is your day?
D. Give me a call.

⑫ _____
A. I told you so.
B. I hope you didn't tell anyone.
C. You told me that last night.
D. Apart from you, no.

⑬ _____
A. I had a headache.
B. I can tell.
C. I will not hurt you.
D. I can't hear you.

⑭ _____

A. Don't overload yourself with work.

B. Don't worry. You did a good job.

C. What are you waiting for? Go for it!

D. I have applied for a job. What about you?

⑮ _____

A. He is in stable condition.

B. I am a surgeon.

C. I have to check other patients.

D. He is doing well in school.

第三部份：簡短對話 🎧 Track 10

共 10 題，每題請聽音檔播出一段對話及一個相關的問題後，從試題冊上 A、B、C、D 四個選項中選出一個最適合者作答。每段對話及問題只播出一遍。

⑯ _____

A. She is surprised to hear that.

B. She feels sorry about that.

C. She doesn't mean it.

D. She doesn't care what he did.

⑰ _____

A. It was great. He met some old friends.

B. It couldn't be better. He bought a pair of shoes.

C. He went shopping with his old friends.

D. He didn't do anything special.

⑱ _____

A. Make a list of all the essays he has to finish on time.

B. Tell him the pros and cons of being an organized person.

C. Start arranging his work schedule as soon as possible.

D. Decide which are the most important things and handle them first.

⑲ _____

A. Buy her father a sewing kit.

B. Buy her father a book on saving money.

C. Buy her father a kitten.

D. Buy her father a shaver.

⑳ _____
A. They can go to the Netherlands together.
B. She can speak Dutch to the waiter.
C. Each of them will pay for their own meal.
D. The man comes from a Dutch family.

㉑ _____
A. He has been to London.
B. He needs some time to change his clothes.
C. He wants to live his life in a different way.
D. It's time for him to move to another city.

㉒ _____
A. Teresa was upset that he got the award.
B. Teresa didn't win the award.
C. Teresa got an award he thought he deserved.
D. Teresa presented him an award.

㉓ _____
A. The man bought a cat from a pet shop.
B. Tiger is a puppy with orange fur.
C. They would go to an animal hospital first.
D. The woman can't keep a dog as a pet.

㉔ _____

Reservation Form		
	Wednesday	**Thursday**
6:30 p.m.	Mr. White	Ms. Woods
7:30 p.m.	Mrs. Black	Mr. Wang

A. Wang.
B. Black.
C. Woods.
D. White.

㉕ _____

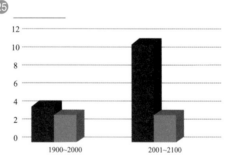

A. 3.
B. 4.
C. 11.
D. 21.

第四部份：簡短談話 🎧 Track 11

共 10 題，每題請聽音檔播出一段談話及一個相關的問題後，從試題冊上
A、B、C、D 四個選項中選出一個最適合者作答。每段談話及問題只播
出一遍。

㉖ _____

A. To give a warning.

B. To make an apology.

C. To show concern.

D. To impose a punishment.

㉗ _____

A. A park.

B. A clothing store.

C. A gym.

D. A concert.

㉘ _____

A. On the descent.

B. After take-off.

C. Prior to boarding a plane.

D. At the immigration desk.

㉙ _____

A. Not to walk their dogs outside.

B. To take their dogs with them after shopping.

C. Not to bring their dogs into the supermarket.

D. The beauty salon is open until 11 p.m.

㉚ _____

A. Improved the environment.

B. Eliminated corruption.

C. Reduced unemployment.

D. Increased spending on schools.

㉛ _____

A. It makes your body feel better.

B. It takes years off you.

C. It helps prevent wrinkles.

D. It saves your time.

㉜ _____

A. They are a married couple.

B. She is his boss.

C. She is the new client.

D. They used to be a couple.

㉝ _____

A. Only used cars.

B. New and second-hand cars.

C. Brand new cars only.

D. Just electric cars.

㉞ _____

A. He used not to read to his children.

B. He is already a father.

C. He wants a child.

D. His wife reads to his children.

㉟ _____

Prohibited Items	
Liquids	○ (Less than 100 ml)
Walking Sticks	○
Dried Food	○
Scissors / Knives	✕

A. Walking sticks.

B. Sharp objects.

C. Bread.

D. 80 ml of body lotion.

閱讀能力測驗

本測驗分三部份，全為四選一之選擇題，共 35 題，作答時間 45 分鐘。

第一部份：詞彙

共 10 題，每題含一個空格。請由試題冊上的四個選項中選出最適合題意的字或詞作答。

1 _____ should you reveal this secret to others.

    A. Seldom   B. Little   C. Never   D. Hardly

2 Dr. Webber is _____ the death of his patient.

    A. essential for   B. necessary for   C. responsible for   D. difficult for

3 Thousands of protesters _____ roads near City Hall for six hours.

    A. were blocking   B. will block

    C. had blocked   D. have been blocking

4 Joanna is a very _____ actress who has played many different characters in movies.

    A. tolerant   B. brutal   C. versatile   D. consequent

5 There is no _____ that this oil painting is a masterpiece.

    A. to deny   B. denies   C. denied   D. denying

6 Stanley might be too young to play professional basketball, but he has great _____.

    A. resistance   B. potential   C. improvement   D. devotion

7 If it had not been for Ken's encouragement, I _____ given up my career.

    A. have been   B. would have   C. will be   D. should

8 Jason's essay _____ some similarities to Sarah's essay.

    A. keeps   B. bears   C. makes   D. veils

9 Mark raised his hand and asked the teacher to _____ the point he just mentioned.

    A. clarify   B. combine   C. comfort   D. calculate

10 I like to sit in a coffee shop and _____ people on the street.

    A. observe   B. offend   C. browse   D. ban

第二部份：段落填空

共 10 題，包括二個段落，每個段落各含 5 個空格。請由試題冊上四個選項中選出最適合題意的字或詞作答。

Questions 11–15

The first postage stamp was beautifully designed. It had a ___(11)___ of the reigning Queen of England, Victoria, on it. It was called the Penny Black because it was black and cost one penny. The Penny Black had a dramatic effect. It changed the world of ___(12)___, just like email did today. ___(13)___ the introduction of the Penny Black, millions more letters were written and sent each year. This was because almost ___(14)___. In our modern world, email has ___(15)___ it possible for people to communicate with each other even more quickly and cheaply than the first postage stamp did.

_____ ⑪ A. rubber   B. passport   C. profile   D. storm

_____ ⑫ A. communication   B. technology

        C. imagination   D. magic

_____ ⑬ A. Before   B. After   C. While   D. Whenever

_____ ⑭ A. someone could endure it   B. somebody could stand it

        C. nobody could blame it   D. everyone could afford it

_____ ⑮ A. makes   B. making   C. made   D. to make

Questions 16–20

The Russian word "Ziferblat" literally means "clock face" in English. It is also the first ___(16)___ of a Russian coffee chain in the United Kingdom. The shop's ___(17)___ pricing strategy takes London by storm. Coffee, food, and snacks ___(18)___. Customers only have to pay for the time they spend there. When customers walk into the shop, they are given an alarm clock to ___(19)___ the time they spend eating and socializing here. To attract more customers, it provides cozy atmosphere and light music to help customers relax. People cannot only bring their own food and drinks here, but also make it in the coffee shop. However, customers have to ___(20)___ after themselves before they go. Does it sound like a good place to kill time to you?

_____ ⑯ A. branch   B. colony   C. choice   D. priority

_____ ⑰ A. normal   B. common   C. innovative   D. political

_____ ⑱ A. are longer provided for free   B. are provided at no charge

          C. are worth a fortune   D. cost a small fortune

_____ ⑲ A. waste   B. change   C. save   D. note

_____ ⑳ A. catch up   B. pick up   C. make up   D. set up

第三部份：閱讀理解

共 15 題，包括數篇短文，每篇短文後有 2~4 個相關問題。請由試題冊上四個選項中選出最適合者作答。

Questions 21–23

Although times are changing, Saudi Arabia remains a traditional society. If the government has its way, people wishing to get married in this country will have one more rule to follow: they will have to go to school before they can become husband and wife.

The government's plan is to teach couples what married life is all about before allowing men and women to take such a big step. Certain classes will focus on what legal rights husbands and wives have, as well as their duties to each other and to their children. Other classes will give helpful advice on how to deal with family conflicts. Still others will teach couples how to communicate effectively since communication is the key to a happy marriage.

The government hopes that it will cut down on the number of Saudis getting divorced. While the government can't control whether or not a marriage is a happy one, the hope is that education will help people make wise decisions to choose a life partner.

_____ ㉑ What's the function of education that is mentioned in the passage?

A. To break up the partnership successfully.

B. To teach students how to make friends with people.

C. To make wise decisions about a life partner.

D. To go to school before we get married.

㉒ According to the passage, what's the key to a happy marriage?

A. Conflicts.   B. Social status.

C. Fortune.   D. Communication.

㉓ The school provides some helpful advice except _____.

A. the legal rights of husband and wife

B. how many children a couple should have

C. how to communicate effectively

D. how to deal with family conflicts

Questions 24–25

The Amazon Rainforest has been described as the "lungs of the planet" because it provides an essential environment for recycling carbon dioxide into oxygen.

Despite the growing international concern, the Amazon Rainforest is being destroyed every single minute. More and more rainforests are lost every day with tragic consequences of both developing and industrial countries. Experts estimate that the last remaining rainforests could be consumed in the near future.

The problem of the destruction of the rainforest and its solution have much to do with the local economy. The rainforest is being destroyed for the profits it yields. Most people see the need to protect the remaining forest while at the same time the need to improve the lives of the people who depend on it. If managed properly, the rainforests can provide for many of the world's needs continuously because forest resources are renewable. Around the world, environmentalists are taking action to save the unique forest before it is too late.

㉔ What does the word "consequence" possibly mean?

A. Result.   B. Accident.   C. Damage.   D. Difference.

㉕ What is the best title for this passage?

A. The Amazon Rainforest—Wonderful Life Form

B. The Amazon Rainforest—Magic but in Danger

C. Amazing Amazon River

D. The History of the Amazon Rainforest

Questions 26–28

Studies show that negative attitudes, thoughts, and emotions can lower the body's immune system. However, positive ones like love, happiness, and laughter can boost the body's immune system. Scientists have found proof that laughter can help fight colds and relieve stress.

One way to add more laughter to your life is by giving laughter yoga a try. Laughter yoga originally started in 1995. It was Dr. Madan Kataria, a doctor from India, initially developed it. It may be an unusual therapy, but it is now practiced in many countries, and it is even catching on in Taiwan.

Laughter yoga is easy to do. It needs neither props nor a good sense of humor. All you just need is laugh. What's more, you do not need a good reason to laugh, you just need a willingness to laugh. This is because the body cannot tell if the laughter is fake or genuine, so the benefits are the same.

26 What is this article mainly about?

A. Ways to make life easier.

B. A good reason to laugh.

C. Laughter is the best medicine.

D. Special treatment in Taiwan.

27 Which of the following weakens the body's immune system?

A. Cheerfulness.

B. Satisfaction.

C. Happiness.

D. Depression.

28 Which of the following statements is true?

A. When doing laughter yoga, you need some tools.

B. There is no evidence that we can benefit from laughter.

C. Dr. Kataria is the founder of laughter yoga.

D. Our body can tell the difference between real laughter and fake laughter.

Dear Mr. Huang,

    I'm writing this letter to you since I'm a big fan of yours, and you have had a great and positive impact on me. I have learned a lot from your actions and words. For example, every time you are determined to do something, you often devote your time and energies to achieve your goal. Once I scored low on my Chinese exam, you told me to persist in it and keep on studying. You have given me not only wings to pursue my dreams but also weapons to fight for victory.

    Since you were infected with the serious flu last week, I prepared some herbal candy for you, hoping that you would recover soon. Though you have had such great passion in teaching, I hope that you can stay healthy and keep on influencing us and improving our academic performance. Hope to see you back to school soon.

Sincerely,

David Chang

㉙ What is true about Mr. Huang and David Chang's relationship?

    A. They are family who live together.

    B. They are classmates who scored low on their exams.

    C. Mr. Huang is David's boss.

    D. Mr. Huang is David's teacher.

㉚ What does David mean to express in the second paragraph of the letter?

    A. To explain his action.   B. To show his support.

    C. To express his appreciation.   D. To share his opinion.

㉛ Where does Mr. Huang probably stay now?

A.   B.   C.   D.

Questions 32–35 are based on information provided in the following advertisement and email.

Winter Holidays

Spend your holidays in Australia.

Enjoy another different summer vacation.

Four people for only NT$88,888

Price Includes:

▶ Air fares   ▶ Two five-star hotel rooms

▶ All transfers   ▶ Theater tickets

Special departures from Dec. to Feb.

Book the trip immediately!

For more information, please contact us.

Sanmin Travel Agency

Tel: 534-1300

Website: https://www.sanmintravel.com.tw

Email: travel@sanmin.com.tw

From: **sophie@mail.com**

To: **travel@sanmin.com.tw**

Subject: **Winter Holidays**

To whom it may concern,

Three friends of mine and I are interested in the trip "Winter Holidays." We think the price is attractive, but we are wondering if tips are all included in the price. Our ideal departure time is around Christmas. Please let us know if it is still available during that time. Thank you so much!

Sincerely yours,
Sophie

32 Who will be most likely attracted by the advertisement?

    A. People who live in Australia.

    B. People who live in New Zealand.

    C. People who love freezing weather.

    D. People who live in the United States.

33 What is **NOT** included in the price?

    A. Main meals.   B. Plane tickets.

    C. Accommodations.   D. Transportation in Australia.

34 Which is **NOT** a way of contacting Sanmin Travel Agency?

    A. By email.   B. By phone.   C. By fax.   D. On the website.

35 If Sophie and her friends book the trip, when will they set off?

    A. In November. B. In December. C. In January.   D. In February.

寫作能力測驗

第一部份：中譯英

說明：請將下列的一段中文翻譯成通順、達意且前後連貫的英文。

　　我叔叔在一家特殊中心上班。他是一名樹醫生。照顧樹木是他每天的工作。他需要收集植物的種子和採集葉子，然後加以研究。當樹木生病時，他也要治療它們。

_____

_____

_____

_____

第二部份：英文作文

說明：請依下面所提供的文字提示寫一篇英文作文，長度約120字（8至12個句子）。作文可以是一個完整的段落，也可以分段。（評分重點包括內容、組織、文法、用字遣詞、標點符號、大小寫。）

提示：雖然我們學習英文有一段時間了，但是或多或少都會遇到困難。為了克服這些困難，請說明你做了哪些努力。

_____

_____

_____

_____

_____

_____

_____

_____

_____

口說能力測驗

請在 15 秒內完成並唸出下列自我介紹的句子：
My seat number is (座位號碼後 5 碼), and my registration number is (考試號碼後 5 碼).

第一部份：朗讀短文

請先利用一分鐘的時間閱讀下面的短文，然後在二分鐘內以正常的速度，清楚正確的讀出下面的短文，閱讀時請不要發出聲音。

It's very difficult to pursue art as a career. Many artists struggle to support themselves financially and may not have any success until late in life or even after death. However, true artists have no choice but to follow their passion. For them, creating art is as necessary as eating or sleeping whether that art finds an audience or not.

* * *

People that have had the misfortune to require emergency medical treatment at a hospital emergency room would tell you that a visit to an emergency room can be more distressing than the medical emergency itself. A growing problem with the emergency department is that the majority of visits are for nonurgent cases, and only a small percentage is actually serious enough to require life-saving treatment.

第二部份：回答問題 🎧 Track 13

共十題。題目已事先錄音，每題經由耳機播出二次，不印在試卷上。第一至五題，每題回答時間 15 秒；第六至十題，每題回答時間 30 秒。每題播出後，請立即回答。回答時，不一定要用完整的句子，但請在作答時間內盡量的表達。

第三部份：看圖敘述  Track 14

下面有一張圖片及四個相關的問題，請在一分半鐘內完成作答。作答時，請直接回答，不需將題號及題目唸出。

首先請利用 30 秒的時間看圖及問題。

1. 這是什麼地方？
2. 照片裡的人在做什麼？
3. 照片裡的人心情看起來如何？請進一步說明。
4. 如果你還有時間的話，請盡可能描述詳細一點。

請將下列自我介紹的句子再唸一遍：

My seat number is (座位號碼後 5 碼), and my registration number is (考試號碼後 5 碼).

全民英檢模擬試題 中級 TEST 3

聽力測驗

閱讀能力測驗

寫作能力測驗

口說能力測驗

聽力測驗

本測驗分四部份，全為四選一之選擇題，共 35 題，作答時間約 30 分鐘。

第一部份：看圖辨義 🎧 Track 15

共 5 題，試題冊上有數幅圖畫，每一圖畫有 1～3 個描述該圖的題目，每題請聽音檔播出題目以及四個英語敘述之後，選出與所看到的圖畫最相符的答案，每題只播出一遍。

A. Question 1

Answer ❶ _____

B. Questions 2 and 3

Answer ❷ _____ ❸ _____

C. **Question 4**

Answer ④ _____

D. **Question 5**

No.	Causes	Percentage *(approximation)*	
Domestic Ranking **The top 5 causes of death**			
1	Cancer	29%	
2	Heart Disease	12%	
3	Stroke	7%	
4	Pneumonia	6%	
5	Diabetes	4%	

Answer ⑤ _____

第二部份：問答 🎧 Track 16

共 10 題，每題請聽音檔播出一英語問句或直述句之後，從試題冊上 A、B、C、D 四個回答或回應中，選出一個最適合者作答。每題只播出一遍。

⑥ _____
A. Of course, it has various functions.
B. No, it's not for sale.
C. It's the only one I have.
D. Yes, I'm an editor.

⑦ _____
A. I don't know what happened.
B. Yes, I can fix it for you.
C. Call the operator now.
D. Sure. First, turn on the power here.

⑧ _____
A. The activity was well-organized.
B. To help save the earth by cleaning up the beach.
C. Yes, we'd like you to join us.
D. It is good to make a contribution.

⑨ _____
A. We haven't found anyone yet.
B. Don't worry about Bill. He will find a new job.
C. The replacement parts are here.
D. You can replace the camera with a cellphone.

⑩ _____
A. I am a student.
B. Your hairstyle is attractive.
C. The pink dress looks pretty on you.
D. It looks more professional.

⑪ _____
A. Insert the coins and push the button.
B. Close the door and turn the key in the lock.
C. Pop the cork and pour some wine for guests.
D. Chop the garlic and stir it into the mixture.

⑫ _____
A. I loved your recommendation.
B. I think I need to see a dentist.
C. Sure, what's your favorite food?
D. Yes, the store is near the town.

⑬ _____
A. There are too many shops.
B. We have too many pets for sale.
C. We open at 10 a.m.
D. It's Christmas Eve.

⑭ _____

A. It's no big deal.

B. No, they're still mad at me.

C. We should close that deal.

D. Yes, a deal is a deal.

⑮ _____

A. Yes, the jet crashed.

B. I can't fly a jet.

C. No, I've been here for a few days already.

D. No, the doctor didn't say anything about my leg.

第三部份：簡短對話 🎧 Track 17

共 10 題，每題請聽音檔播出一段對話及一個相關的問題後，從試題冊上 A、B、C、D 四個選項中選出一個最適合者作答。每段對話及問題只播出一遍。

⑯ _____

A. She talks too much, and it bothers Jennifer.

B. She is very polite to all of her colleagues.

C. She is annoyed by the man's questions.

D. She has to finish her work at a particular time.

⑰ _____

A. He is a web page designer.

B. He is awaiting the outcome of the test.

C. He is having a job interview.

D. He is interviewing a candidate for the job.

⑱ _____

A. Linda's aunt.

B. The bakery.

C. The woman's aunt.

D. The man's aunt.

⑲ _____

A. Buy him a newspaper from a stand.

B. Get some paper from the market.

C. Leave him outside the market.

D. Wait for him outside the market.

⑳ _____

A. The woman liked to eat hamburgers.

B. They've known each other since college.

C. Michael Bates had a nickname in high school.

D. The man didn't know who Michael Bates was.

43

㉑ _____

A. He failed his exams.

B. He gets poor grades.

C. His girlfriend is breaking up with him.

D. His girlfriend is not gentle and generous.

㉒ _____

A. His calculator is broken.

B. Something went wrong with the calculations.

C. His numbers are too big.

D. The woman didn't check the numbers.

㉓ _____

A. She's having problems with her computer.

B. She doesn't know how to use a computer.

C. She can't find the file she needs on the computer.

D. She's not satisfied with her report.

㉔ _____

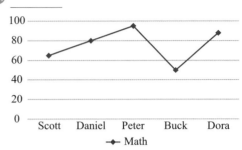

A. Scott.

B. Daniel.

C. Peter.

D. Buck.

㉕ _____

Floor Guide

3F	Men's Wear	
2F	Sporting Goods	
1F	Women's Wear	
B1F	Supermarket	

A. B1F.

B. 1F.

C. 2F.

D. 3F.

第四部份：簡短談話 🎧 Track 18

> 共 10 題，每題請聽音檔播出一段談話及一個相關的問題後，從試題冊上 A、B、C、D 四個選項中選出一個最適合者作答。每段談話及問題只播出一遍。

㉖ _____
A. He is calling from the park.
B. He is probably a responsible dog owner.
C. He is the host for the call-in show.
D. He is happy on the show.

㉗ _____
A. She is badly injured.
B. Her body temperature is too high.
C. She fainted in the heat.
D. She was attacked and panicked.

㉘ _____
A. Soups and side dishes.
B. Rice and noodles.
C. Bread and cakes.
D. Drinks.

㉙ _____
A. He owes her client money.
B. He is mentioned in his aunt's will.
C. He is planning to move house.
D. He is being sued by his aunt.

㉚ _____
A. They make you feel lonely.
B. They are interesting in the office.
C. Our enemies can use them to fight.
D. The majority of them are untrue.

㉛ _____
A. She is opening a science museum.
B. She is analyzing some fossils in Japan.
C. She is giving a guided tour in the museum.
D. She is giving a presentation on all living creatures.

㉜ _____
A. Use it every day, and you will have a fresh taste.
B. You won't have tooth decay if you use it.
C. It can cure bad breath after using a while.
D. It is better than just brushing your teeth.

㉝ ______

A. The boss of the amusement park will make an announcement.

B. Engineers will take a look at the roller coaster.

C. The amusement park will be closed today.

D. The families of the victims will visit the park.

㉞ ______

A. Tells users the names of the planets.

B. Finds out where certain stars are.

C. Tells users their horoscopes.

D. Takes photos of the night sky.

㉟ ______

HOT PIZZA

Small: $10

Large: $15

Toppings ($2 per topping):

Ham / Beef / Shrimp / Salmon / Green pepper / Pineapple / Broccoli

A. Meat.

B. Seafood.

C. Fruit and vegetables.

D. All of the above.

第一部份：詞彙

共 10 題，每題含一個空格。請由試題冊上的四個選項中選出最適合題意的字或詞作答。

1. The police officer was _____ about what the suspect said. He didn't believe that the suspect was innocent.

   A. believable   B. unbelievable   C. trustful   D. doubtful

2. Do you know if there is any shop nearby _____ I can get a pair of shoes?

   A. as   B. while   C. where   D. which

3. The truth about the whole thing is about to _____ . Soon, the public will know more about what really happened.

   A. merge   B. emerge   C. conceal   D. confess

4. The adventurer always tends to _____ when people ask him about his life in the Amazon jungle.

   A. cooperate   B. demonstrate   C. immigrate   D. exaggerate

5. It is time that you _____ fooling around and concentrated on your studies.

   A. stops   B. stopped   C. stopping   D. stop

6. It _____ rain tomorrow, but I'm not sure.

   A. can   B. may   C. be   D. must

7. Keeping early hours is _____ to one's health.

   A. financial   B. official   C. beneficial   D. special

8. Only when you become a parent yourself _____ the difficult situations your parents have encountered when they raised you.

   A. you realize   B. do you realize

   C. you realize how   D. and then you realize

9. A training _____ for new employees will be held in the conference room next weekend.

   A. device   B. facility   C. session   D. catalogue

⑩ Vicky is cautious about spending her money so she is not _____ to buy something unnecessary.

A. like   B. likely   C. unlike   D. likewise

第二部份：段落填空

共 10 題，包括二個段落，每個段落各含 5 個空格。請由試題冊上四個選項中選出最適合題意的字或詞作答。

Questions 11–15

What do you know about Colombia? It is a country ___(11)___ in the northwest of South America. Nearly one third of the country's population ___(12)___ in poverty. Some People are even forced to live on the streets. Fortunately, the government has been able to help these people because the country has experienced some economic ___(13)___. For example, the Mayor of Bogotá, Colombia's capital, launched a program to help the city's needy. The program provided the homeless with portable bathrooms so that they could have a refreshing bath. These portable bathrooms could be used by ___(14)___. The homeless also get basic medical care after ___(15)___ a bath. According to the authorities, the program is so successful that it will be held again.

⑪ A. located   B. locates   C. locating   D. to locate

⑫ A. living   B. are living   C. to living   D. lives

⑬ A. depression   B. growth   C. policy   D. trend

⑭ A. millions of pets a day   B. thousands of rich people a day

     C. hundreds of people a day   D. most of officials a day

⑮ A. taken   B. took   C. taking   D. takes

Questions 16–20

Look around your house, and you will probably see soap, washing powder, glue, paint, and other household items. But did you know that ___(16)___ and died because they were used to test these products?

Every year, countless animals are used to test different products. Laws in most countries do not require that these items ___(17)___ tested on animals. However, the law ___(18)___ state that products must be safe for humans and must not damage the environment. Therefore, many companies use animal testing. They believe that it will protect them ___(19)___ lawsuits. If a product hurts someone, a company can claim that the product has been tested on animals.

Today, companies continue to make "new and improved" products, but many people wonder ___(20)___ the new products and animal testing are really needed.

⑯ A. lots of students endured   B. a large number of people stood

     C. quite many species bore   D. thousands of animals suffered

⑰ A. be   B. being   C. are   D. will be

⑱ A. didn't   B. doing   C. do   D. does

⑲ A. with   B. from   C. when   D. that

⑳ A. which   B. if   C. what   D. when

第三部份：閱讀理解

共 15 題，包括數篇短文，每篇短文後有 2~4 個相關問題。請由試題冊上四個選項中選出最適合者作答。

Questions 21–23

During puberty, hormone levels in a teenager's body will change. This causes acne, sometimes called pimples or zits. Though acne is common, there are many misconceptions about it.

The first mistake many people make is popping their pimples. This only presses germs into the skin, causing redness and even infection. Next, some people mistakenly believe that eating greasy food or chocolate causes pimples. This is untrue because a balanced diet is still important. Another misconception is that stress causes acne. Stress does make your skin produce more oil, but this does not create more pimples. However, you shouldn't wash your face too much because this can irritate your skin.

A final misconception about acne is that make-up causes it. Actually, special acne-fighting medicine is found in most make-up today. Though there are many misconceptions about acne, one thing is for certain: consult a doctor about the treatment that works best for you.

_____ ㉑ What is the passage mainly about?

A. Reasons why pimples appear during puberty.

B. Tips to reduce pimples.

C. Common misunderstandings about pimples.

D. How make-up does harm to your skin.

_____ ㉒ According to the passage, which of the following is the main reason why pimples appear during puberty?

A. Putting up make-up every day.

B. Too much fried food in the diet.

C. Too much stress in daily life.

D. The hormonal changes in teenagers' body.

_____ ㉓ What can we conclude from this passage?

A. When you have acne, the best way to solve it is to consult a doctor.

B. If you have pimples, pop them and they will be gone.

C. Greasy food won't cause acne, so eat as much greasy food as you can.

D. Putting on make-up can prevent acne.

Questions 24–26

Volunteering my time and professional skills is important to me for many reasons. The most important reason is that I feel it is necessary to contribute to society by helping others. For me, it makes perfect sense to do this by offering my writing and public relations services to non-profit organizations that help others. Being a volunteer makes me feel good that I can help a person or organization that is in need. Furthermore, I have been very lucky in my life and feel it's important to share that good luck with others who may not have an easy life. Last but not least, volunteering is important to me for business reasons. Companies and clients are always judging the people working for them, and it's essential to look good in their eyes. I have gotten a lot of satisfaction from volunteering, and it's important to me for these reasons.

_____ ㉔ Which of the following is **NOT** a reason for the author to do volunteering job?

    A. To help people in need.   B. To share good luck with others.

    C. To get satisfaction from it.   D. To earn more money.

_____ ㉕ How does the author help others?

    A. Offering his or her writing and public relations services to non-profit organizations.

    B. Donating money to non-profit organizations.

    C. Sharing with others how miserable he or she is.

    D. Working for companies and clients without receiving payment.

_____ ㉖ Which of the following is closest in meaning to the word "volunteer"?

    A. Helping others with your profession.

    B. Doing something without receiving anything in return.

    C. Getting satisfaction from what you are doing.

    D. Sharing memorable things with others.

Questions 27–29

If you want your children to get better grades, will you pay them to hit the books? Should international corporations pay for the right to pollute the environment we live in? Is it moral to pay people to try new and dangerous drugs? Can prisoners pay for getting a better cell?

Michael J. Sandel, Harvard professor, discusses these questions in his book *What Money Can't Buy: The Moral Limits of Markets*. He also mentions one of the tricky questions of our time: Is there anything wrong that everything has a price tag on it? And, if **so**, what can we do to prevent the price from going sky-high? What about the moral values of markets?

In recent years, we can find that the market value for everything, including education, government, medicine, even personal relations, is out of control. It seems that money plays a more important role than ethic in the society. Is this where we want to be? He hopes that his book can <u>provoke</u> readers into thinking the difficult question: what should be the role of money and markets in our societies?

㉗ From which of the following is the passage likely to be taken?

A. 　B. 　C. 　D.

㉘ What does the word "**so**" in the second paragraph refer to?

A. To look for a price tag on a product.

B. To answer the difficult question.

C. To mention moral standards.

D. To pay for everything.

㉙ The word "provoke" in the last paragraph is closest in meaning to _____.

A. arouse　　　B. persuade　　　C. escape　　　D. transform

Questions 30–32

One day, the police came to the hospital where Dr. Paul Grout worked and arrested him for buying child pornography online. Paul denied the charges, but the police didn't believe him. After the arrest, the police went to Paul's house and searched his house and computers. They found no illegal pornography. Even so, Paul went to trial for buying illegal pornography because the police said his credit card records proved he had bought the illegal photos. Luckily, the doctor was able to prove—based on his work records—that he couldn't have possibly purchased the photos on the Internet. He was not even near computers at the times some of the photos were purchased. The police eventually discovered that someone had stolen Paul's "identity" and was using his credit card numbers to commit crimes. This terrible story shows the dangers of identity theft and how it can ruin your life.

30 Why was Dr. Paul Grout being arrested?

A. He was believed to have killed his patient.

B. He was believed to have killed a child.

C. He was believed to have stolen someone's identity online.

D. He was believed to have bought illegal photos on the Internet.

31 What happened when the police searched Dr. Paul Grout's computer?

A. They found illegal photos in his computer.

B. They found that Dr. Paul Grout stole other's identity.

C. They found that Dr. Paul Grout was a thief.

D. They found no criminal evidence in Dr. Paul Grout's computer.

32 Which of the following descriptions is **NOT** correct?

A. Dr. Paul Grout was innocent.

B. The work records proved that Dr. Paul Grout was guilty.

C. Somebody stole Dr. Paul Grout's credit card information.

D. Dr. Paul Grout worked in a hospital.

Questions 33–35

HEALTH MARKET

Special Sale!

Prices and quality, you can trust!

Open 7 Days, 10 A.M.–11 P.M.

Honeycrisp Apples 99 ¢ /lb.	Jumbo Navel Oranges 2 lbs for $3.	Ripe Hass Avocados 3 for $1.	Sweet Yellow Peaches 98 ¢ /lb.
Sweet Honey Mangos 2 for $1.	Large Beefsteak Tomatoes 98 ¢ /lb.	Whole Seedless Watermelons $3 ea.	Green Seedless grapes 89 ¢ /lb.

DO YOU KNOW?

We have more than 300 varieties of scoopable nuts, grains, beans, cereals in every store. Just get a bag, find the item you want, and fill the bag as much or as little as you want! Please notice that no mixing!

For more information, please visit *healthmarket.com* or call 357-2100.

SALE PRICES ARE VALID FROM 9/9 TO 9/18 IN ALL STORES.

_____ ㉝ If you want to buy 3 watermelons, 2 mangos, and 4 lbs of oranges, how much should you pay?

A. 7 dollars.　　B. 11 dollars.　　C. 14 dollars.　　D. 16 dollars.

_____ ㉞ Which of the following about the foods in Health Market is **NOT** true?

A. There are many options to choose from.

B. Customers can scoop as much as they need.

C. You can put everything you need in the same bag.

D. It is available for every branch of Health Market.

_____ ㉟ Which of the following statements is true?

A. It will cost you 89¢ if you want to buy a pound of grapes on September 8th.

B. Customers can buy every product at a discount this year.

C. Health Market has confidence in its price and quality.

D. You can download an app to check more details about Health Market.

寫作能力測驗

第一部份：中譯英

說明：請將下列的一段中文翻譯成通順、達意且前後連貫的英文。

　　在加拿大時，我和肯尼是鄰居並上同一所小學。那時我們常一起打籃球、玩線上遊戲，度過許多快樂時光。畢業以後，我和家人移居到臺北。從此我們就以電子郵件彼此連絡。

_____

_____

_____

_____

第二部份：英文作文

說明：請依下面所提供的文字提示寫一篇英文作文，長度約120字（8至12個句子）。作文可以是一個完整的段落，也可以分段。（評分重點包括內容、組織、文法、用字遣詞、標點符號、大小寫。）

提示：上個月，山姆的朋友余 (Yu) 姓夫婦邀請他到臺東 (Taitung) 做客。現在，請你以山姆的身份寫信給他們，謝謝他們的招待，並描述當你在臺東作客時令你印象深刻的事情。另外，也邀請他們到你位於臺北的家中拜訪。

_____

_____

_____

_____

_____

_____

_____

_____

_____

口說能力測驗

🎧 Track 19

請在 15 秒內完成並唸出下列自我介紹的句子：
My seat number is (座位號碼後 5 碼), and my registration number is (考試號碼後 5 碼).

第一部份：朗讀短文

請先利用一分鐘的時間閱讀下面的短文，然後在二分鐘內以正常的速度，清楚正確的讀出下面的短文，閱讀時請不要發出聲音。

Doctors say that water is better than sports drinks. They recommend that people drink about eight ounces of water thirty minutes before exercising. Then, drink four to eight ounces of water every fifteen minutes while exercising and about eight ounces after a workout.

*　　　　　　　*　　　　　　　*

Korean TV series now have lots of fans in many countries. They are aired during prime time, and many people hurry home just to watch them. Stories of love triangles, everyday family affairs, kings and queens, and doctors are very popular. Fans say they love their good-looking idols, the latest fashions they wear, and so on.

第二部份：回答問題 🎧 Track 20

共十題。題目已事先錄音，每題經由耳機播出二次，不印在試卷上。第一至五題，每題回答時間 15 秒；第六至十題，每題回答時間 30 秒。每題播出後，請立即回答。回答時，不一定要用完整的句子，但請在作答時間內盡量的表達。

下面有一張圖片及四個相關的問題，請在一分半鐘內完成作答。作答時，
請直接回答，不需將題號及題目唸出。

首先請利用 30 秒的時間看圖及問題。

1. 這是什麼地方？
2. 這張照片給你怎麼樣的感覺？
3. 你覺得這張照片裡面的環境是很安靜還是很吵呢？請進一步說明。
4. 如果尚有時間，請說明你對這個環境的看法。

請將下列自我介紹的句子再唸一遍：

My seat number is (座位號碼後 5 碼), and my registration number is (考試號碼
後 5 碼).

全民英檢模擬試題 中級 TEST 4

聽力測驗

閱讀能力測驗

寫作能力測驗

口說能力測驗

聽力測驗 ▌ 本測驗分四部份，全為四選一之選擇題，共 35 題，作答時間約 30 分鐘。

第一部份：看圖辨義 🎧 Track 22

共 5 題，試題冊上有數幅圖畫，每一圖畫有 1～3 個描述該圖的題目，每題請聽音檔播出題目以及四個英語敘述之後，選出與所看到的圖畫最相符的答案，每題只播出一遍。

A. Question 1

Answer ❶ _____

B. Question 2

Answer ❷ _____

60

C. Question 3

Answer ③ _____

D. Questions 4 and 5

Answer ④ _____ ⑤ _____

第二部份：問答 🎧 Track 23

共 10 題，每題請聽音檔播出一英語問句或直述句之後，從試題冊上 A、
B、C、D 四個回答或回應中，選出一個最適合者作答。每題只播出一遍。

⑥ _____

A. The final exam was last week.

B. No, it wasn't your fault.

C. Yes, I did very well.

D. I'm in seventh grade.

⑦ _____

A. He is around the corner.

B. I've never heard of that guy.

C. I'm not leaving without him.

D. Where have you been, Eric?

⑧ _____

A. I have to make ends meet.

B. You can have as much as you want.

C. It cost me ten thousand dollars.

D. That depends on how many days we
will stay in Tokyo.

⑨ _____

A. Beats me.

B. Trust me! It won't happen again.

C. Thank you for your consideration.

D. They are my cousins. Haven't I told
you before?

⑩ _____

A. It's Saturday, so I can't make it to
your party.

B. We'll go to bed at nine o'clock.

C. It starts on the first Monday of June.

D. Neither. It's on the twenty-first.

⑪ _____

A. I regret to tell you that you are not
hired.

B. What have you done to him?

C. No. I think you are doing a great
job.

D. What's that supposed to mean?

⑫ _____

A. Relax! It is just a game.

B. You know I am not a quitter.

C. Everyone can participate in the
game.

D. I know. You can call me anytime.

⑬ _____

A. Yesterday was great.

B. Sure, I'll be there.

C. I can't wait to meet her.

D. The meeting was held at nine.

⓮ _____

A. There's a post office nearby.

B. How much money did you spend?

C. Why? The deadline was last week.

D. Mr. Lee will have two children.

⓯ _____

A. I'm proficient in Japanese now.

B. I'm very excited and I can't wait to visit there.

C. It was fantastic! I had a tremendous time.

D. It was horrible, and I would never go to that restaurant again.

第三部份：簡短對話 🎧 Track 24

共 10 題，每題請聽音檔播出一段對話及一個相關的問題後，從試題冊上 A、B、C、D 四個選項中選出一個最適合者作答。每段對話及問題只播出一遍。

⓰ _____

A. He thought everyone would like ice cream.

B. His wife is an excellent cook.

C. The ice cream was made by himself.

D. He believed that a cup of water is better than ice cream.

⓱ _____

A. Four o'clock.

B. Four thirty.

C. Five o'clock.

D. Five thirty.

⓲ _____

A. She likes beef.

B. She hates fish.

C. For religious reason.

D. For no reason.

⓳ _____

A. To become the athletic director.

B. To train a handball team.

C. To take a long vacation.

D. To retire from basketball.

⓴ _____

A. She is questioning the man.

B. She is very nervous about it.

C. She hates exams.

D. She is not nervous at all.

㉑ _____

A. Tim should be sent home immediately.

B. Tim needs more examination.

C. Tim has to take some pills.

D. Tim needs surgery.

㉒ _____

A. The weather is wet.

B. The weather is warm.

C. The weather is cold.

D. The weather is hot.

㉓ _____

A. He can't think of a good title.

B. He is too busy to write a book.

C. He is having a hard time with the ending.

D. He needs advice about his book's ending.

㉔ _____

NOTES

· Sunshine Café: Yummy food

· Moon Restaurant: Worth to go

· Kitten Kitchen: Ideal location

· Life BAR: High price

A. Sunshine Café.

B. Moon Restaurant.

C. Kitten Kitchen.

D. Life BAR.

㉕ _____

A. They're free until January 1st.

B. They're not available until next month.

C. They're cheaper this year.

D. They're not valid next year.

第四部份：簡短談話 🎧 Track 25

共 10 題，每題請聽音檔播出一段談話及一個相關的問題後，從試題冊上 A、B、C、D 四個選項中選出一個最適合者作答。每段談話及問題只播出一遍。

㉖ _____

A. Warn the animals.

B. Open their sunroofs.

C. Honk their horns.

D. Keep within the speed limit.

㉗ _____

A. The special offer starts tomorrow.

B. The customers are not interested.

C. The offer ended yesterday.

D. It has run out of hamburgers.

㉘ _____

A. He gives a talk for free.

B. He is a famous brain surgeon.

C. He won't attend the talk today.

D. He wrote a book about the human brain.

㉙ _____

A. Pick up Jimmy in Taipei.

B. Take the bus instead.

C. Pay for Jimmy's gas.

D. Call Jimmy when she arrives.

㉚ _____

A. They should turn on the electric light.

B. They should turn off their cellphones.

C. They should take out the garbage.

D. They should unfasten their seat belts.

㉛ _____

A. Someone gambled at cards.

B. Mr. Chang has been kidnapped.

C. International terrorists have been found.

D. Crimes have been committed.

㉜ _____

A. She quit eight years ago.

B. She gave him the award.

C. She gave him help and advice.

D. She should have won the award.

㉝ _____

A. Following the tour guide.

B. Seeing the exhibit.

C. Chewing gum.

D. Taking photos.

㉞ _____

A. It's next to the office.

B. It's near their mom's house.

C. They are already there.

D. Sam went there before.

㉟ _____

Skinny Quick Tea

Drink 6 cups every day!
Buy here!
www.skinnyquicktea.com
Only NT$888 per box!
Make You Young and Beautiful!

A. How much Skinny Quick Tea you
should drink.

B. Where people can buy Skinny
Quick Tea.

C. How much a box of Skinny Quick
Tea is.

D. Whether Skinny Quick Tea is safe.

閱讀能力測驗

本測驗分三部份，全為四選一之選擇題，共 35 題，作答時間 45 分鐘。

第一部份：詞彙

共 10 題，每題含一個空格。請由試題冊上的四個選項中選出最適合題意的字或詞作答。

1 _____ the novel sold millions of copies, it didn't win high praise from literary critics.

   A. As a result   B. Although   C. In a word   D. Regardless of

2 People respond _____ to stress. Some take it calmly while others don't.

   A. sincerely   B. incredibly   C. apparently   D. differently

3 Joe spends the _____ of his time on video games.

   A. authority   B. majority   C. capacity   D. curiosity

4 _____ it not for my wife's assistance, I would not get over the difficulties.

   A. Were   B. If   C. Had   D. Without

5 Today, most office workers _____ computers more than ever to do their work.

   A. move over   B. tear down   C. live up to   D. rely on

6 All of us were _____ when we heard that one of our neighbors had been broken into last night.

   A. shy   B. proud   C. shocked   D. spoiled

7 The church served as a _____ refuge for the flood victims.

   A. temporary   B. technological   C. timid   D. tolerable

8 You _____ told Amelia your secret. She is a big mouth!

   A. should   B. shouldn't   C. shouldn't have   D. should have

9 The old man was threatened by some gangsters to _____ all his money from the bank.

   A. gamble   B. withdraw   C. overthrow   D. establish

10 Dr. Blake is an excellent surgeon, and all the doctors in this hospital are looking forward to _____ with her.

   A. work   B. working   C. works   D. worked

第二部份：段落填空

共 10 題，包括二個段落，每個段落各含 5 個空格。請由試題冊上四個選項中選出最適合題意的字或詞作答。

Questions 11–15

Taipei 101 is the tallest building in Taiwan. It is ___(11)___. Frequent earthquakes, wind and rain brought by strong typhoons are its main ___(12)___. Therefore, C.Y. Lee, one of the designers of Taipei 101, had to make sure the building was ___(13)___ to endure harsh weather conditions in Taiwan. The building has extreme flexibility, which can prevent imbalanced movement and ensure structural integrity (完整). This kind of ___(14)___ makes sure people who work and live in the building are safe. In addition, the curtain walls enhance critical structural elements, ___(15)___ the building firmer and more stable.

_____ ⓫ A. a peace settlement in different ways

  B. a big commitment to people at the moment

  C. a full-time employment in the area

  D. an architectural achievement in many levels

_____ ⓬ A. challenges B. difficulties C. consequences D. quarrels

_____ ⓭ A. high enough B. enough high C. strong enough D. enough strong

_____ ⓮ A. acceptance B. resistance C. circumstance D. substance

_____ ⓯ A. making B. is making C. to make D. made

Questions 16–20

Which class is suitable for you? Some experts believe that students in a smaller class may be less likely to have a passive attitude ___(16)___ learning. Students may become actively involved when ___(17)___. Their listening skills can be improved greatly if they ___(18)___ well with their teachers and their peers. ___(19)___, teachers are able to do their jobs better because this allows them to find out who learns well before exams, not after. However, running a class like this is not easy for teachers. It needs energy, imagination, and commitment and all of ___(20)___ are exhausting. It is a lot of hard work, but it is worth it.

_____ ⓰ A. from B. toward C. in D. against

⑰ A. there are only a few students in the class

　　 B. all parents go to work on time

　　 C. their teachers quit their jobs

　　 D. the principal treats them to lunch

⑱ A. establish　　　　B. discuss　　　　C. argue　　　　D. interact

⑲ A. As a result　　　　　　　　B. Even though

　　 C. On the other hand　　　　D. In contrast

⑳ A. who　　　　B. which　　　　C. what　　　　D. where

第三部份：閱讀理解

共 15 題，包括數篇短文，每篇短文後有 2~4 個相關問題。請由試題冊上四個選項中選出最適合者作答。

Questions 21–23

　　Having problems with your career or your love life? The followers of the ancient Chinese philosophy feng shui will tell you that the root of your problems may be the design of your home.

　　The ultimate goal of feng shui is to achieve harmony between human beings and their environment. The philosophy of feng shui recommends, for example, having green plants and beautiful decorations to make your environment pleasant, or keeping your working environment clean can increase your ability to work. Another piece of advice—placing your furniture in order that you won't be sitting or sleeping with your back to the door—originates from those times when people lived in fear of a wild animal or an enemy coming through the door. Some people still have that instinct for being uncomfortable when they can't observe the entrance while resting.

　　Today, feng shui is widely practiced not only by Chinese, but by people around the world. Many celebrities have become fans of feng shui. Banks and office buildings are built and decorated according to the principles of this ancient Chinese philosophy. Feng shui books are sold worldwide, and feng shui consultants have their offices in many countries. People all over the world intend to use feng shui to bring peace and harmony to their surroundings.

_____ ㉑ What is the purpose of this article?

A. To tell the difference between western culture and eastern culture.

B. To live in harmony with the environment.

C. To introduce an ancient medical cure.

D. To explain how to make the world peaceful.

_____ ㉒ The word "surroundings" in the last paragraph is closest in meaning to _____ .

A. ability   B. future   C. philosophy   D. environment

_____ ㉓ What can be inferred from this article?

A. Some people believe that feng shui has influence on their lives.

B. Sleeping with your head to the door is good feng shui.

C. People can buy feng shui books in China only.

D. Keeping your house clean can reduce your ability.

Questions 24–25

The summer vacation has come to an end, and it is time to go back to school and hit the books. Would you like to adapt some new study techniques to improve your academic performance this new school year? A survey found that many of our old study habits may not be as effective as we thought they were.

Take the idea of studying in the same place, for example. A research indicates that you may learn more effectively if you study in two or more places. In a similar way, researchers now believe that it is better to study different but related things at a time, instead of concentrating intensely on just one thing. Although conventional wisdom has it that "immersion" is the best way to master something, these findings seem to show that our brains find deeper connections and learn more effectively when presented with a variety of related things.

So, this school year, consider studying in more than one place as well as studying a variety of things at one time. These new study techniques, paired with personal motivation and hard work, may be just what is needed to enable you to learn more effectively.

_____ ㉔ According to the passage, which of the following is true?

A. The most efficient way to study is to focus on one thing only.

B. Only when new school year is coming can you start studying.

C. Research has shown that most students use the right way to study.

D. Studying in different places helps you learn things more effectively.

_____ ㉕ According to this article, who will do the best in his or her field?

A. Mike, who learns English only by listening to radio.

B. Annie, who always hits the book in different places.

C. John, who lacks motivation to learn Japanese.

D. Peggy, who always prepares for her final exams in the library.

Questions 26–28

Running over 42 kilometers, the marathon is the longest race of the Olympic Games. But actually, many other marathons are also held around the world every year. There are many famous race in the world such as the Boston Marathon, London Marathon, and Chicago Marathon—almost every major city in the world organizes a marathon for various reasons. In Taiwan, we have the Taipei Marathon and the rather famous Taroko Gorge Marathon, where the runners accomplish a challenging task—running through a gorge.

Today, the marathon honors not only a great Greek runner, but the strength, determination, and courage of human beings. It requires extreme physical fitness, endurance, and mental strength. It also represents the true spirit of Olympics or any competitions. Winning or losing does not matter; participating in the race and finishing it is more important—as it symbolizes the spirit of humanity.

_____ ㉖ Which of the following descriptions about the marathon is **NOT** true?

A. The marathon is the longest race of the Olympic Games.

B. There are only 3 major cities organizing the marathons.

C. The Taroko Gorge Marathon is famous for its challenging task.

D. The marathon requires extreme physical endurance.

_____ ㉗ One who wants to participate in a marathon needs _____.

A. lots of money   B. native tongue

C. mental strength   D. Greek nationality

_____ ㉘ According to the passage, what is the true spirit of the marathon?

A. Winning or losing.   B. Running as fast as you can.

C. Participating in and finishing it.   D. Running through a gorge.

Questions 29–31

Taroko Gorge

Day Tour

Departs daily from Hualien at 9:30 a.m. & back in Hualien at 5:30 p.m.

OPEN ALL YEAR LONG

Pickups available from Hualien Airport and Hualien Train Station.

This Deluxe Bus Tour Includes:

· Tunnel of Nine Turns

· Eternal Spring Shrine

· Swallow Grotto

· Cihmu Bridge

· Buluowan

· Baiyang Trail

***Free Time in Tienhsiang for Lunch, Sightseeing, Shopping, and Other Attractions Nearby.

Sale Prices!

NT$1,000

Child Under 12: NT$800

Lunch Included Buffet at the Sanmin Restaurant—Worth NT$500!

10% discount for groups of 15 or more people!

★Full Insurance Included★

Online Reservation: https://www.sanmintaroko.com.tw/daytour/

or Reserved by Phone at: 654-3200

㉙ Which of the following is **NOT** included in this Taroko Gorge Day Tour?

A.

B.

C.

D.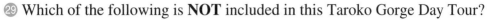

㉚ Anyone can join the tour except _____ .

A. a six-year-old little girl

B. a tourist who arrives in Hualien at 10 a.m. and intends to leave at 3 p.m.

C. a backpacker who wants to enjoy the scenery of Taroko Gorge

D. a family that hopes to travel trough Taroko Gorge without driving their car

㉛ If there is a group of 20 people including 4 children under the age of 12 who want to join this day tour, they should pay _____ in total.

A. NT$20,000

B. NT$19,200

C. NT$17,280

D. NT$16,000

Questions 32–35 are based on information provided in the following advertisement and email.

Flower Hotel
NOW HIRING!

Position: Head Baker

Job Description:

We are looking for an experienced head baker with at least 7 years of experience in the field. You will be responsible for preparing and baking bread and cakes, arranging the display case, and creating new baked goods. It is also the head baker's responsibility to make an order for more ingredients if the ingredients are running low. This position requires you to follow recipes and meet safety and health regulations as well. We will have an interview with qualified applicants.

CONTACT US!

Ms. Pitts

Human Resources Manager

749-2233 ext. 123

HRM@flowerhotel.com

HOW TO APPLY:

1. Visit "https://www.flowerhotel.com."

2. Click "APPLY NOW."

From: **sarahwu@cmail.com**

To: **HRM@flowerhotel.com**

Subject: **Job application**

Attached: **CV**

Dear Ms. Pitts,

I am interested in the position of head baker at your company. I have eight years of baking experience. I believe my ability qualifies me for the position. If you give me this opportunity, I will definitely help you create new baked goods that cater to the mass market. I have attached my CV, and I look forward to discussing my qualifications with you. Thank you for your consideration.

Sincerely,
Sarah Wu

㉜ What information is **NOT** provided in the advertisement?

    A. How to contact the hotel.   B. How to apply for the position.

    C. What kind of position is offered.   D. Who wants to leave a position.

㉝ What is this email for?

    A. Filling a position.

    B. Looking for a new job.

    C. Pursuing new business opportunities.

    D. Looking for people with baking experience.

㉞ Which of the following is **NOT** a reason why Sarah thinks the hotel should offer her the position?

    A. She has several baking certificates.

    B. She has over seven years of baking experience.

    C. Her ability makes her suitable for the vacant job.

    D. She can create new baked goods for the hotel.

㉟ If the hotel considers offering Sarah the position, what will they probably do next?

    A. Contact Ms. Pitts.

    B. Visit "https://www.flowerhotel.com."

    C. Ask Sarah to send her CV to them.

    D. Have a meeting with Sarah.

寫作能力測驗

第一部份：中譯英

說明：請將下列的一段中文翻譯成通順、達意且前後連貫的英文。

上個週末颱風來襲，我坐在窗邊望著雨水淹滿了街道。突然，我聽到有人大喊：「救命！」原來是有個小男孩掉到水裡去了。我衝出去及時把小孩救了起來。雖然他受了很嚴重的驚嚇，但並沒有放聲大哭。

_____

_____

_____

_____

第二部份：英文作文

說明：請依下面所提供的文字提示寫一篇英文作文，長度約120字（8至12個句子）。作文可以是一個完整的段落，也可以分段。（評分重點包括內容、組織、文法、用字遣詞、標點符號、大小寫。）

提示：全世界每天都有天災人禍不停地發生，包括地震、水災、戰爭、飢荒等，造成很多人流離失所，小孩失去父母。你認為這些人最可憐的原因何在？請說明你的看法。

_____

_____

_____

_____

_____

_____

_____

_____

口說能力測驗

 Track 26

請在 15 秒內完成並唸出下列自我介紹的句子：
My seat number is (複試座位號碼後 5 碼), and my registration number is (初試准考證號碼後 5 碼).

第一部份：朗讀短文

請先利用一分鐘的時間閱讀下面的短文，然後在二分鐘內以正常的速度，清楚正確的讀出下面的短文，閱讀時請不要發出聲音。

London is a classic city with its monuments, bridges, and landmarks. Gradually, I realized what made London such a striking city. Modern London has communities of people from every country. For example, Indians, Russians, Chinese, Australians, French, Irish, and Spanish all have their own social groups.

*   *   *

Winning an Academy Award is the most outstanding achievement in the film industry. Every year the world's attention becomes focused on Hollywood to discover who will win the awards and be guaranteed fame for the rest of their lives. On the night of the ceremony, the entire world is watching.

第二部份：回答問題 Track 27

共十題。題目已事先錄音，每題經由耳機播出二次，不印在試卷上。第一至五題，每題回答時間 15 秒；第六至十題，每題回答時間 30 秒。每題播出後，請立即回答。回答時，不一定要用完整的句子，但請在作答時間內盡量的表達。

第三部份：看圖敘述 🎧 Track 28

下面有一張圖片及四個相關的問題，請在一分半鐘內完成作答。作答時，請直接回答，不需將題號及題目唸出。

首先請利用 30 秒的時間看圖及問題。

1. 這是什麼地方？
2. 這些漂流木和垃圾是怎麼來到這裡的？
3. 這樣的景象帶給你怎樣的感受？
4. 如果尚有時間，請詳細描述圖片中的景物。

請將下列自我介紹的句子再唸一遍：

My seat number is (座位號碼後 5 碼), and my registration number is (考試號碼後 5 碼).

全民英檢 模擬試題 中級 TEST 5

聽力測驗
第一部份　看圖辨義
第二部份　問答
第三部份　簡短對話
第四部份　簡短談話

閱讀能力測驗
第一部份　詞彙
第二部份　段落填空
第三部份　閱讀理解

寫作能力測驗
第一部份　中譯英
第二部份　英文作文

口說能力測驗
第一部份　朗讀短文
第二部份　回答問題
第三部份　看圖敘述

聽力測驗 ▌ 本測驗分四部份，全為四選一之選擇題，共 35 題，作答時間約 30 分鐘。

第一部份：看圖辨義 🎧 Track 29

共 5 題，試題冊上有數幅圖畫，每一圖畫有 1～3 個描述該圖的題目，每題請聽音檔播出題目以及四個英語敘述之後 ，選出與所看到的圖畫最相符的答案，每題只播出一遍。

A. Question 1

Answer ❶ _____

B. Questions 2 and 3

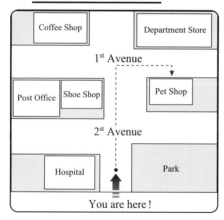

Answer ❷ _____ ❸ _____

C. Question 4

Answer ④ _____

D. Question 5

Answer ⑤ _____

第二部份：問答 🎧 Track 30

共 10 題，每題請聽音檔播出一英語問句或直述句之後，從試題冊上 A、
B、C、D 四個回答或回應中，選出一個最適合者作答。每題只播出一遍。

⑥ _____

A. Doctors make a lot of money.

B. You'd better go to the hospital.

C. I'd like to be a surgeon.

D. I went to consult my family doctor yesterday.

⑦ _____

A. It's Eric Pitts.

B. Oh, he is a college student.

C. He was named after his father.

D. That's my manager's name, too.

⑧ _____

A. We can't make a decision that fast.

B. I will see what I can do.

C. We should make a decision before sunset.

D. I think we should take a vote.

⑨ _____

A. No, I don't think so.

B. He's probably a nice guy.

C. He thinks we are great.

D. Yes, he's good-looking.

⑩ _____

A. Like what?

B. What are you looking at?

C. It's no big deal.

D. Mind your own business.

⑪ _____

A. Her daughter's name is Claire.

B. I think it is Monica.

C. It doesn't have to be signed.

D. Lisa is taller than Monica.

⑫ _____

A. No, it's not fair! I won't do it for you!

B. Sure. Let me show you how it works.

C. May I see your receipt, please?

D. Don't worry. You will find a new one over there.

⑬ _____

A. It was delicate and delicious.

B. Japanese food is my favorite.

C. I suggest you quit smoking.

D. I know a good restaurant nearby.

⑭ _____

A. I didn't want to go either.

B. Are you coming with Lucas?

C. Did he say when?

D. He is a member of the cast.

⑮ _____

A. It's your favorite flavor, isn't it?

B. What kind of favor is that?

C. Oh, no. You have a fever.

D. Here you are. You can thank me later.

第三部份：簡短對話 🎧 Track 31

共 10 題，每題請聽音檔播出一段對話及一個相關的問題後，從試題冊上 A、B、C、D 四個選項中選出一個最適合者作答。每段對話及問題只播出一遍。

⑯ _____

A. It was not open yet.

B. It went out of business.

C. It was under construction.

D. It changed its menu four hours ago.

⑰ _____

A. Japanese cuisine.

B. Beef noodles.

C. In their room.

D. A guidebook.

⑱ _____

A. She thinks they are very interesting.

B. She thinks they make fast movements.

C. She's seen them in fantasy movies.

D. She finds them disgusting.

⑲ _____

A. She wore a new watch.

B. She carried a new bag.

C. She bought a new necklace.

D. She dyed her hair.

⑳ _____

A. The man may fall ill.

B. This is a teaching hospital.

C. The man was afraid to go to the hospital.

D. Because the woman was stubborn.

㉑ _____

A. Pretend that she didn't know them.

B. Act like a superstar.

C. Buy a new car.

D. Change her appearance.

㉒ _____

A. Heavy traffic.

B. A late pizza delivery.

C. He is a delivery man.

D. The man brought the wrong pizza.

㉓ _____

A. Set multiple records at a time.

B. Break into a house.

C. Release a new album.

D. Stop a record from being made.

㉔ _____

A. The man needs to do the shopping.

B. The man is bothering the woman.

C. The woman gives the man a ride.

D. The woman doesn't want the man to wait for her.

㉕ _____

A. The library.

B. The restaurant.

C. The playground.

D. The supermarket.

第四部份：簡短談話 🎧 Track 32

共 10 題，每題請聽音檔播出一段談話及一個相關的問題後，從試題冊上 A、B、C、D 四個選項中選出一個最適合者作答。每段談話及問題只播出一遍。

㉖ _____

A. Sell them to a second-hand bookstore.

B. Give them away to charities.

C. Keep them and give him someone else's books.

D. Put them in boxes and recycle them.

㉗ _____

A. Recycling, green energy and pollution are not taught at school.

B. Most people know nothing about environmentally friendly companies.

C. By buying green products, people have the power to improve the environment.

D. If we want to change the world, we have to spend all our money.

㉘ _____

A. Strangers like it.

B. It's popular.

C. Shy people use it.

D. It's a skill.

㉙ _____

A. Parents should not ignore their children.

B. Technology is our enemy most of the time.

C. Smartphones should be avoided in early childhood.

D. Children don't pay attention like they used to.

㉚ _____

A. They will take another plane.

B. They will take a train to India.

C. They will take the same plane once it has been fixed.

D. They will take a plane arranged for the following day.

㉛ _____

A. Ignore what doctors used to say about sunshine.

B. Avoid being in the sun as much as possible.

C. Allow ourselves to get some sunshine.

D. Try to keep our skin beautiful.

㉜ _____

A. Before he went to Africa.

B. While he was learning to be a writer.

C. After quitting his job as a doctor.

D. About twenty years ago.

㉝ _____

A. They can get their money back.

B. Take a train to the bus station.

C. Change platforms to take a train.

D. Book another train ticket.

㉞ _____

A. Women who like to shop for luxury goods.

B. Someone with a limited budget.

C. Teenagers who have their own credit cards.

D. Someone who can't afford a smartphone.

㉟ _____

> **Jackson's Gym**
> *Open from 7 a.m. to 9 p.m. every day!*
> We are equipped with:
> * Weighing Scales   * Lockers
> * Snack Bars   * Shower Rooms
> Keep fit and relax at Jackson's Gym!

A. Taking a shower is not allowed at the gym.

B. The gym is open less than 9 hours a day.

C. There is a swimming pool at the gym.

D. People can buy some food at the gym.

閱讀能力測驗
本測驗分三部份，全為四選一之選擇題，共 35 題，作答時間 45 分鐘。

第一部份：詞彙

共 10 題，每題含一個空格。請由試題冊上的四個選項中選出最適合題意的字或詞作答。

❶ Both my family and colleagues suggest that I _____ several days off and take a vacation abroad.

A. was taken　　B. take　　　C. am taking　　D. took

❷ To _____ harming her unborn baby, Kelly quit drinking and smoking during pregnancy.

A. ascend　　B. approach　　C. assure　　D. avoid

❸ On seeing Nathan's wonderful performance on stage, his parents cannot but _____.

A. cries　　B. crying　　C. to cry　　D. cry

❹ Simon was fired by his boss for _____ his duty.

A. locating　　B. spotting　　C. neglecting　　D. resembling

❺ Amanda _____ reality by reading romances and watching romantic comedy films.

A. escapes　　B. features　　C. defends　　D. inspires

❻ Sarah _____ into tears when she heard the news that her childhood friend died in a car accident.

A. ran　　B. burst　　C. twisted　　D. gripped

❼ We are not able to access the website _____ it is now under construction.

A. though　　B. despite　　C. as　　D. from

❽ We can have a picnic beside the river _____ the weather is fine.

A. as well as　　B. as long as　　C. as far as　　D. as good as

❾ The job is _____ easy so I think we should be able to finish it this afternoon.

A. recklessly　　B. exclusively　　C. relatively　　D. readily

_____ ⑩ _____ Kelly gone to the movie with us last night, she could have bumped into her favorite actor, Jack.

A. If   B. Had   C. Should   D. Were

第二部份：段落填空

共 10 題，包括二個段落，每個段落各含 5 個空格。請由試題冊上四個選項中選出最適合題意的字或詞作答。

Questions 11–15

Understanding different cultures is important. After two people start dating, their cultural backgrounds usually determine ___(11)___ quickly the romantic relationship can progress. In the United States, physical contact, such as hugging and kissing, ___(12)___ common very early in the relationship. In Korea, ___(13)___, kissing is not considered proper for at least several weeks. ___(14)___, parents also play an important role in cross-cultural relationships. Although they might say that their children are free to date whoever they choose, parents often ___(15)___.

_____ ⑪ A. where   B. when   C. what   D. how

_____ ⑫ A. is   B. are   C. will be   D. have been

_____ ⑬ A. furthermore   B. in addition   C. on one hand   D. on the other hand

_____ ⑭ A. At first   B. For instance   C. Apart from that   D. In other words

_____ ⑮ A. suffer huge losses late in life

     B. discourage their relatives to marry late

     C. pretend to their colleagues that nothing has happened

     D. put pressure on their children to date someone from their own culture

Questions 16–20

To play in the National Basketball Association (NBA) is the dream of many young basketball players. In order to fulfill this dream, they practice harder and harder, even push their bodies to the ___(16)___. All of their efforts will pay off when they hear their names called at the annual NBA draft.

Isaiah Austin, an American young basketball player, is completely blind ___(17)___ his right eye. He had overcome many difficulties to enter the NBA draft.

Unfortunately, just four days before the draft started, he was ___(18)___ with Marfan syndrome, a rare disease that could kill him during vigorous exercise. Therefore, Isaiah announced that he could no longer play basketball at a competitive level since it ___(19)___. This devastating news ended his playing career. However, the NBA decided to do something to make up for that. Isaiah was invited to the draft. Much to his ___(20)___, he was offered a job in the NBA and could still be involved in the game.

_____ ⑯ A. deadline   B. frontier   C. limit   D. boundary

_____ ⑰ A. in   B. on   C. under   D. with

_____ ⑱ A. negotiated   B. diagnosed   C. connected   D. supplied

_____ ⑲ A. served as a warning to others   B. made a contribution to charity

    C. brought peace to the world   D. posed a risk to his life

_____ ⑳ A. annoyance   B. dismay   C. surprise   D. regret

第三部份：閱讀理解

共 15 題，包括數篇短文，每篇短文後有 2~4 個相關問題。請由試題冊上四個選項中選出最適合者作答。

Questions 21–23

In the United Kingdom, a woman suffering from terminal brain disease wanted her husband to help her die. The woman couldn't kill herself because she was too weak to control her body. Unfortunately, her husband would go to jail for murder if he helped her. The woman said this violated her human rights. A similar argument happened in the United States. A woman was unconscious for many years. Her husband wanted to turn off the machines that kept her body alive, but the woman's parents said no even though she was brain-dead. The husband sought legal help, but it took him fifteen years to win. Finally, they decided to let the woman die peacefully.

Many people regard mercy killing as unacceptable, so governments will not legally protect it. However, this is beginning to change. A few countries now recognize living wills, which tell doctors and family members that you want to die if the disease you have can't be cured.

_____ ㉑ What did the American woman's husband want to do?

    A. To turn off the machines that kept his wife's body alive.

B. To kill his wife and then commit suicide.

C. To put his wife in jail.

D. To do whatever it takes to save his wife.

22 The word "terminal" in first paragraph is closest in meaning to _____.

    A. criminal   B. serious   C. fatal   D. infectious

23 According to the passage, which of the following statements is true?

    A. The British woman had suffered from brain death and was kept alive by machines.

    B. It took the American woman's husband fifty years to win the right to turn off his wife's life support machine.

    C. In some countries, the doctor can perform mercy killing based on the patient's living wills.

    D. A healthy person can choose mercy killing to end his or her own life.

Questions 24–26

We all have to speak in front of a large group of people in some situations. The situation may be a company meeting, an academic conference, a wedding or a funeral. Most people are usually quite nervous about their speaking skills and stage performances. For those of us who need extra practice or self-confidence, there are some organizations that can help us to gain confidence in public speaking.

The Carnegie training program includes a series of group sessions that teach students how to develop self-assurance, positive attitudes and poise in public speaking. The program emphasizes clear speaking, logic, and enthusiasm for delivering a speech in public. In this way, the listening audience will remain interested and become informed. Some groups such as the Rotary Club also offer members opportunities to practice their public speaking skills. There are also other chances to speak in most schools, such as student associations and debate competitions.

Learning how to manage your fears and gaining self-confidence are essential skills for great public speakers. If you wish to become one of them, try to take advantage of the organizations and opportunities mentioned above. Last but not least, practice makes perfect.

24 This article is mainly about _____.

    A. ways to help you improve your public speaking skills

B. the trend to take the Carnegie training program

C. several tips to convey right message to right people

D. when is the best time to speak properly

_____ ㉕ The word "enthusiasm" in the second paragraph is closest in meaning to

_____ .

    A. fear   B. passion   C. courage   D. determination

_____ ㉖ According to the article, what can we learn from the Carnegie training program?

    A. Innovation.   B. Investment.   C. Management.   D. Confidence.

Questions 27–29

Imagine you are in your kitchen cooking, and you glance at the counter for the next step in the recipe. A well-known chef says, "Now add a pinch of salt and stir." You do this, and then you touch the tablet to move to next step in the interactive cooking lesson. You then reach into the oven to take out the fish that is being cooked. But when your oven mitt contact the dish, it says "It's not ready. Please wait for a few minutes."

This might appear in a science-fiction movie, but it's actually a project carried out by a small group of researchers. They are focusing on the place where we spend so much time—the kitchen. Their goal is to build a smart kitchen that makes cooking an easy thing for everyone. For example, the refrigerator will tell you whether food stocks are low and what should be purchased from stores; a coffee maker will inform you when it is the right temperature to have a cup of coffee. All of the kitchen facilities can be worked with a combination of sensors and computers to make your kitchen a more enjoyable place to work. You can even be able to cook dishes you never dreamed of.

Some intelligent kitchen appliances are not quite ready for the market because of their prices. However, this kitchen technology will be affordable in the future one day.

㉗ This article is mainly about _____ .

    A. the intelligent kitchen appliances

    B. a new cooking lesson

    C. an interactive cooking video

    D. a successful cooking team

㉘ According to the article, which of the following statements is true?

    A. The kitchen technology will be cheaper in the future.

    B. There's a faster way to cook fish.

    C. Kitchen is combined with a play area.

    D. Cooking will become extremely complicated.

㉙ What is the author's attitude toward smart kitchen?

    A. Indifferent.   B. Negative.   C. Optimistic.   D. Skeptical.

Questions 30–32

> To Whom It May Concern,
>
>   My name is Thomas Jefferson. I am a 22-year-old graduate. I would like to apply for the job advertised in *The Express* newspapers as an engineer.
>
>   My career ambition is to work as an engineer. I believe the study I have recently finished will help me with this work. At school, I got high grades in mathematics and computer design. I also studied professional engineering, which I enjoyed greatly.
>
>   Briefly, I am a well-organized and hardworking person. I can be reached at any time at the phone number or email address listed on my résumé. I am available to start working immediately. Thank you for your interest and time.
>
>   Yours sincerely,
>
>   Thomas Jefferson

㉚ What kind of letter is this one?

    A. A letter of recommendation.   B. A letter of application.

    C. A letter of resignation.   D. A thank-you letter.

㉛ According to the letter, what qualification may **NOT** be required to be an engineer?

    A. Being well-organized and diligent.

    B. Being good at math and computer design.

C. An interest in engineering.

D. A master's degree in Literature.

㉜ Which of the following statements about Thomas Jefferson is true?

A. He plans to go to graduate school in Seattle.

B. He majors in chemistry at collage and wants to be a scientist.

C. He can be contacted by both phone and email.

D. He won't be able to start working until next month.

Questions 33–35

You are invited to

Joyce Lee's Clothing Store

ANNUAL SALE

Joyce Lee is a label known for its women's wear including 100% wool sweater, well cut jeans, floral dress and must-have bag. It is also a label famous for its amazing annual sale in Taipei. We are offering 50% off all women's wear and 25% off all the bags. You can get an extra 10% on all items if you spend more than NT$500. Please make a note of the following information:

Date: December 15th～December 31st

Time: 10 a.m.～9 p.m.

We look forward to seeing you there!

㉝ Which of the following items is **NOT** sold in *Joyce Lee's Clothing Store*?

A. 　　B. 　　C. 　　D.

㉞ How much do you need to pay for a NT$600 bag after discount?

A. NT$405.　　B. NT$250.　　C. NT$450.　　D. NT$375.

㉟ Which of the following statements is true?

A. *Joyce Lee's Clothing Store* is located in Japan.

B. *Joyce Lee's Clothing Store* is on sale for 15 days.

C. *Joyce Lee's Clothing Store* has sales three times a year.

D. A man's jacket can't be found in *Joyce Lee's Clothing Store*.

寫作能力測驗

第一部份：中譯英

說明：請將下列的一段中文翻譯成通順、達意且前後連貫的英文。

　　每天晚上我挑燈夜戰，盡一切努力準備考試。然而，無論我多麼用功讀書，每天的時間似乎總是不夠。我經常到凌晨二、三點才睡覺。因為缺乏睡眠，所以我上課時常感到疲憊不堪。

_____

_____

_____

_____

Writing

第二部份：英文作文

說明：請依下面所提供的文字提示寫一篇英文作文，長度約120字（8至12個句子）。作文可以是一個完整的段落，也可以分段。（評分重點包括內容、組織、文法、用字遣詞、標點符號、大小寫。）

提示：現代人生活忙碌，適時的休息和放鬆顯得格外重要。請寫下利用短短幾分鐘時間就能休息放鬆的步驟。

_____

_____

_____

_____

_____

_____

_____

_____

_____

口說能力測驗

🎧 **Track 33**

請在 15 秒內完成並唸出下列自我介紹的句子：

My seat number is (座位號碼後 5 碼), and my registration number is (考試號碼後 5 碼).

第一部份：朗讀短文

請先利用一分鐘的時間閱讀下面的短文，然後在二分鐘內以正常的速度，清楚正確的讀出下面的短文，閱讀時請不要發出聲音。

Many modern expressions began with the daily habits of people who lived a long time ago. For example, the saying "knock on wood" came from a very old superstition. Centuries ago, people believed that spirits lived in wood. Whenever they felt in danger, they would knock on wood to call good spirits for protection.

*　　　　　　　*　　　　　　　*

The word "cosplay" is a combination of two English words: "costume and play." Cosplay is something fun that people all over the world can do. In cosplay, people dress up to look like their favorite characters from books, video games, movies, and comic books. There are many events and shows around the world that people dress in costume. Many of these costumes can be very elaborate and are handmade. Cosplay has been happening since 1980s and has been a growing hobby ever since that time. Today, it is very popular and many people dress up for fun.

第二部份：回答問題 🎧 Track 34

共十題。題目已事先錄音，每題經由耳機播出二次，不印在試卷上。第一至五題，每題回答時間 15 秒；第六至十題，每題回答時間 30 秒。每題播出後，請立即回答。回答時，不一定要用完整的句子，但請在作答時間內盡量的表達。

下面有一張圖片及四個相關的問題，請在一分半鐘內完成作答。作答時，請直接回答，不需將題號及題目唸出。

首先請利用 30 秒的時間看圖及問題。

1. 照片裡的人在什麼地方？
2. 照片裡的人在做什麼？
3. 你覺得照片裡的人開心嗎？你是如何得知的？
4. 如果尚有時間，請詳細描述圖片中的景物。

請將下列自我介紹的句子再唸一遍：

My seat number is (座位號碼後 5 碼), and my registration number is (考試號碼後 5 碼).

全民英檢模擬試題 中級 TEST 6

聽力測驗
第一部份　看圖辨義
第二部份　問答
第三部份　簡短對話
第四部份　簡短談話

閱讀能力測驗
第一部份　詞彙
第二部份　段落填空
第三部份　閱讀理解

寫作能力測驗
第一部份　中譯英
第二部份　英文作文

口說能力測驗
第一部份　朗讀短文
第二部份　回答問題
第三部份　看圖敘述

聽力測驗

本測驗分四部份,全為四選一之選擇題,共 35 題,作答時間約 30 分鐘。

第一部份:看圖辨義 🎧 Track 36

共 5 題,試題冊上有數幅圖畫,每一圖畫有 1～3 個描述該圖的題目,每題請聽音檔播出題目以及四個英語敘述之後 , 選出與所看到的圖畫最相符的答案,每題只播出一遍。

A. Question 1

Answer ❶ ＿＿＿＿

B. Question 2

Answer ❷ ＿＿＿＿

C. Questions 3 and 4

Answer ③ _____ ④ _____

D. Question 5

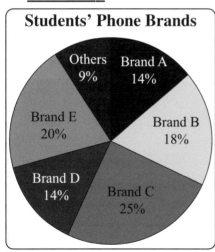

Answer ⑤ _____

第二部份：問答 🎧 Track 37

共 10 題，每題請聽音檔播出一英語問句或直述句之後，從試題冊上 A、B、C、D 四個回答或回應中，選出一個最適合者作答。每題只播出一遍。

⑥ _____

A. Ten percent will be enough.

B. He doesn't need our advice.

C. The bill wasn't so expensive.

D. I can offer you a tip for saving money.

⑦ _____

A. It was not a date! It was a night out with a friend.

B. Great. He helped me set a date for the meeting.

C. Perfect. He is the best candidate for the job.

D. Rick said the closing date for applications is May 6th.

⑧ _____

A. Three months later.

B. I haven't seen you for a long time.

C. It opens at 9 a.m.

D. I haven't heard anything about the location yet.

⑨ _____

A. It has two bedrooms, one kitchen, and one bathroom.

B. It's a five-story building.

C. It took one year to complete.

D. It's near the downtown.

⑩ _____

A. Fill out the form and sign here.

B. Call the room service and then ask for a towel.

C. Sorry, I don't have a clue!

D. Maybe you can tell me how to get it.

⑪ _____

A. With a little effort, we might.

B. If you come, yes.

C. It's always on time.

D. Being on time is a great virtue.

⑫ _____

A. I think Tokyo will be great.

B. I had to take a taxi there.

C. I went to Paris.

D. I'll go to the beach on Tuesday.

⑬ _____

A. How dare you!

B. Have a nice day.

C. Don't run in the hallway.

D. How is she doing in the new company?

⑭ _____

A. They live near the sea.

B. I think steak is a better choice.

C. I'll see them off at five.

D. They don't eat pork chops.

⑮ _____

A. OK. Is 10 a.m. convenient for you?

B. It is just your excuse for being late.

C. I will tell them to send the letter to your work address.

D. No. No one can talk him into changing his mind.

第三部份：簡短對話 🎧 Track 38

共 10 題，每題請聽音檔播出一段對話及一個相關的問題後，從試題冊上 A、B、C、D 四個選項中選出一個最適合者作答。每段對話及問題只播出一遍。

⑯ _____

A. Her knees are sore because of jogging.

B. She doesn't like to swim.

C. Her favorite exercise is doing yoga.

D. She prefers swimming to jogging.

⑰ _____

A. Go out and get some fresh air.

B. Take some stuff out.

C. Open a window.

D. Find someone else.

⑱ _____

A. He thinks his neighbor is a terrible piano player.

B. He doesn't want to hear that sound anymore.

C. He plays the piano better than his neighbor.

D. He wishes that he could hear a different one.

⑲ _____

A. Read all chapters of the book.

B. Do exercises of the next chapter.

C. Hand in their assignments.

D. Prepare for a quiz on the next chapter.

⑳ _____

A. She lives very close to her grandparents.

B. She is too busy to visit her grandparents often.

C. Her grandparents visit her often.

D. She lives with her parents and grandparents.

㉑ _____

A. An expensive watch.

B. People on earth.

C. The price tag.

D. The oil price.

㉒ _____

A. Lisa went to the drugstore.

B. The man went to the drugstore.

C. The woman went to the drugstore.

D. Nobody went to the drugstore.

㉓ _____

A. Detective novel.

B. Historical novel.

C. Romance fiction.

D. Science fiction.

㉔ _____

A. A captain.

B. A flight attendant.

C. A close friend.

D. A taxi driver.

㉕ _____

List
✕ Hairdryer
✕ Beach Towel
✓ Shampoo and conditioner
✓ _____

A. Suntan lotion.

B. Sunglasses.

C. Umbrella.

D. Water bottle.

第四部份：簡短談話 🎧 Track 39

共 10 題，每題請聽音檔播出一段談話及一個相關的問題後，從試題冊上 A、B、C、D 四個選項中選出一個最適合者作答。每段談話及問題只播出一遍。

㉖ _____
- A. She quit her job.
- B. She didn't like her students.
- C. She might take parental leave.
- D. She asked the speaker to take care of her students.

㉗ _____
- A. Taking a walk.
- B. Listening to music.
- C. Baking bread and cookies.
- D. Shopping in a department store.

㉘ _____
- A. The staff are practicing their sales skills.
- B. Someone has made a fire in the building.
- C. There is an emergency in the building.
- D. Someone has called the fire department.

㉙ _____
- A. A poet.
- B. A lawyer.
- C. A chef.
- D. A historian.

㉚ _____
- A. To promote the swimming pool.
- B. To reduce the number of deaths from drowning.
- C. To keep children busy during their summer vacation.
- D. To make swimming a popular summer activity.

㉛ _____
- A. The old people have nowhere to go.
- B. There are too many old people.
- C. There are not enough funds.
- D. The elderly don't use the activity center much.

㉜ _____
- A. He has an excellent memory.
- B. He has passed away.
- C. He is good at telling stories.
- D. He keeps in touch with the speaker.

㉝ _____
- A. At a travel agent.
- B. At an airport.
- C. On a train.
- D. On a ship.

34 _____

A. Visit Wendy at 9 a.m. tomorrow.

B. Wait for Wendy to mail his wallet.

C. Call Simon about this problem.

D. Go to Simon's house tomorrow afternoon.

35 _____

John's Market

1. Buy 5 kinds of organic vegetables and get 40% off.
2. Buy one get one free! All bread!
3. Sign up for our membership now!

Coupons are valid until Oct. 15!

A. There is no discount on bread.

B. Customers can use the coupons all year round.

C. It costs $150 to become a member of the store.

D. People can get a 40% discount on five kinds of organic vegetables.

閱讀能力測驗

本測驗分三部份，全為四選一之選擇題，共 35 題，作答時間 45 分鐘。

第一部份：詞彙

共 10 題，每題含一個空格。請由試題冊上的四個選項中選出最適合題意的字或詞作答。

1 Compared to the climate of the past years, it is _____ warm this year.

    A. sincerely   B. severely   C. relatively   D. enormously

2 Wendy tried to stay calm, but I _____ a slight change in her voice.

    A. encountered   B. distracted   C. detected   D. imitated

3 If the same thing happened to Joe, what would you suggest _____?

    A. him   B. he   C. his   D. to him

4 Craig is going to hold an important meeting tomorrow; _____, he will still go to the concert tonight.

    A. hence   B. likewise   C. nevertheless   D. otherwise

5 I didn't hear the phone ring. I _____ have been fast asleep.

    A. would   B. had to   C. must   D. used to

6 What is the _____ for operating this machine?

    A. research   B. therapy   C. procedure   D. exposure

7 By the time we arrived home, my grandmother _____ dinner. It was time for all of us to enjoy the feast.

    A. were done completing   B. had finished preparing

    C. had finished   D. were completed with

8 Anna's experience in the fashion industry made the interviewer believe that she is the best _____ for the job.

    A. competitor   B. candidate   C. suspect   D. player

9 Everyone in the room was interviewed by Mr. Trump, _____?

    A. weren't they   B. isn't he   C. aren't you   D. was he

10 Ann invited her friends to her party, but _____ were able to come.

    A. little   B. much   C. few   D. less

第二部份：段落填空

共 10 題，包括二個段落，每個段落各含 5 個空格。請由試題冊上四個選項中選出最適合題意的字或詞作答。

Questions 11–15

Roughly 1,400 meters below the surface of the Pacific Ocean near California lived an amazing female octopus. Researchers found a female octopus spent almost five years brooding her eggs. That is longer than any __(11)__ species on the planet. Throughout this period of time, she stayed alert to __(12)__ her eggs from being eaten by other predators. Researchers said that they never saw the female octopus leave her eggs or eat anything. __(13)__, in order to make sure the eggs get enough oxygen, she had to keep the eggs clean and clear away debris from them. Most female octopuses die about the same time after their eggs hatch. These young octopuses were fully __(14)__ surviving on their own after they hatched out thanks to the long brooding period. Otherwise, it might be difficult for them to survive in the deep sea __(15)__. In other words, they could be eaten by other creatures immediately.

_____ ⑪ A. alien   B. known   C. extinct   D. insect

_____ ⑫ A. recover   B. avoid   C. protect   D. insure

_____ ⑬ A. In addition   B. As a result   C. For instance   D. On the contrary

_____ ⑭ A. capable of   B. sensible of   C. convinced of   D. aware of

_____ ⑮ A. from other parents   B. against their parents' wills

         C. with their father's protection   D. without their mother's protection

Questions 16–20

Some parents believe that watching TV is not good for their children. However, it can actually be a(n) __(16)__ tool. The use of TV for learning is to watch programs __(17)__ specifically for education. There are many shows for children and full of good programs about nature, travel, and history on TV. Additionally, TV shows with __(18)__ can help children increase their vocabulary and reading ability. Parents can make __(19)__ TV an educational activity by asking their children to watch the show carefully. After the show, parents can ask children to __(20)__. In this way, children can learn how to organize what they see and hear. Thus, if used correctly, television can be an important part of children's education.

     ⑯ A. software   B. essential   C. research   D. educational

     ⑰ A. written   B. created   C. allowed   D. required

     ⑱ A. gestures   B. visual effects   C. subtitles   D. advertisements

     ⑲ A. watch   B. watches   C. watched   D. watching

     ⑳ A. answer to their prayers

          B. summarize the content of the program

          C. expand the business

          D. have another confrontation

Reading

第三部份：閱讀理解

共 15 題，包括數篇短文，每篇短文後有 2~4 個相關問題。請由試題冊上四個選項中選出最適合者作答。

Questions 21–24

We lift the corners of our mouth. We smile. We don't only smile with our mouth, but also smile with our eyes. It is said that the eyes are the windows of the <u>soul</u>. People can look into our eyes and see our heart.

A smile is a well-known symbol around the world. It represents happiness and shows that our heart is open and that we care for others. It is important for daily communication between people. We learn how to smile when we are babies. We find that when we smile everyone around us smiles too. A smile says that "we are happy and enjoying ourselves." We all understand that a smile brings us good energy. Good energy passes from one person to another.

If we smile at a stranger sometimes, we can make their day better. Maybe they will also smile at someone else. Maybe that person will smile at the next person. The whole world will soon be smiling. Let's do it now!

     ㉑ What is the main idea of this passage?

          A. A smile makes people nervous in your company.

          B. A smile passes energy and makes everyone happy.

          C. A smile makes people feel like a baby.

          D. A smile shows that we don't care about someone.

_____ ㉒ A smile may refer to "_____" in this passage.

A. a close conversation

B. the power of love

C. a way of self-understanding

D. a common expression of enjoyment

_____ ㉓ The word "soul" in the first paragraph means "_____."

A. the thoughts and emotions of a human being

B. the internal organ of a human being

C. the eyes of a human being

D. the quality of something

_____ ㉔ According to the passage, which of the following statements is correct?

A. People don't smile when they grow bigger.

B. Don't smile at people you don't know.

C. Good energy passes from one person to another.

D. The more you smile, the more people you will meet.

Questions 25–26

There is a battle in the world that has been going on longer than any war. Every year around wintertime mankind deals with an attack of the flu virus, also known as influenza, a respiratory disease.

When the human body gets a virus, it usually produces antibodies that protect it from getting that particular form of virus. Unlike many other viruses, the flu virus is not stable and changes each year. Therefore, the earlier acquired protection doesn't work against new viruses unless the change in the virus is very slight. Unfortunately, the flu virus may undergo a big change and major outbreaks take place worldwide. Until now the flu virus is still one of those enemies that people have to learn to fight.

_____ ㉕ The passage is mainly about _____.

A. what the influenza is and how it affects human life

B. how to prevent the influenza

C. why the human body gets influenza

D. where the influenza comes from

26 Why can't people destroy the flu virus thoroughly?

    A. The flu virus is widespread throughout wintertime.

    B. That's because the flu virus is invisible.

    C. The flu virus is not stable and changes each year.

    D. Human body usually produces antibodies to fight against it.

Questions 27–29

Welcome to A New Year

Let's Reminisce!

1. We hit over 57 million users in over 190 countries. We even have two users from Chagos Islands, a narrow strip of land near the Maldives.

2. Our team worked day and night. We consumed more than 7,000 pounds of coffee. We probably drank every type of coffee in the world. Several times over.

3. We were even in a French soap opera. Yep! This really happened.

4. Over one thousand apps were installed over the previous year.

5. More than 250 million new images were uploaded by our users.

6. Our design studio reached a total of 530 stunning templates!

7. Last, there was no error!

---

27 Which of the following might be the reason that they drank every type of coffee in the world several times?

    A. They worked around the clock last year.

    B. They explored the mystery of every type of coffee.

    C. They strived for a contract with a large company.

    D. They will hold an international competition this year.

28 Which of the following statements is true about the team?

    A. The number of their customers was on the decline last year.

    B. A soap opera in the U.S. adopted their design.

    C. Maldivians are their customers.

    D. The team accumulated 530 templates over the previous year.

29 What is the purpose of the list?

    A. To discuss some plans.   B. To set goals for the coming year.

C. To look back on last year.　　　D. To modify the templates.

Questions 30–32

Disneyland has become a tourist attraction since it opened in 1955 in California. It was followed sixteen years later by Walt Disney World in Orlando, Florida. The success of these two very popular theme parks inspired a third: Tokyo Disneyland, which opened to the public in 1983. This Disneyland in Asia is unique in several ways, and it even has a different owner.

Not only is the owner of Tokyo Disneyland different from its two predecessors in America, but the design of the park is different too. In California and Florida, the weather is mild, but in Tokyo it is much more changeable. This **resulted in** replacing Main Street, which is mainly an outdoor area, with a covered World Bazaar at the entrance to the park. There are also many more covered attractions here than at the other parks.

Although Tokyo Disneyland is somewhat different in its design, it has added many of the same experiences that are found at the other two parks in America. With its continuing addition of attractions, Tokyo Disneyland will very likely continue to be successful in the future.

_____ ㉚ What is the reason that Tokyo Disneyland used a covered World Bazaar to replace Main Street?

A. Different climates.

B. Safety regulations.

C. Number of tourists.

D. Government's request.

_____ ㉛ The phrase "**result in**" in the second paragraph is closest in meaning to

_____ .

A. build　　　　B. use　　　　C. introduce　　　D. cause

_____ ㉜ According to the passage, what can we see in Tokyo Disneyland?

A. Many indoor attractions.

B. Warm weather.

C. A garden differs from the others.

D. Many thrilling roller coasters.

are based on information provided in the following poster and instructions.

How to Make a Jack-O'-Lantern

1. Get everything ready. You will need a pumpkin, a knife, a marker, a spoon, a candle, and a lighter.
2. Use a knife to cut off the top of the pumpkin. Don't throw it away.
3. Clean out the inside of the pumpkin.
4. Use the marker to draw a nose, a mouth, and two eyes on the pumpkin.
5. Use a knife to cut through the lines you just drew.
6. Clean the pumpkin.
7. Light a candle with a lighter and place it inside the pumpkin.
8. Put the top of the pumpkin back on, and you now have a jack-o'-lantern of your own!

㉝ According to the poster, what can be learned about the party?

    A. It will be held on October 30th.

    B. People should attend the party at 9 a.m.

    C. People can go to the party for free.

    D. Drinks are available free of charge.

㉞ Who most likely goes to the Halloween party?

A.

B.

C.

D.

㉟ According to the instructions, which of the following is true?

    A. Clean the pumpkin and then use a knife to cut through the lines you just drew.

    B. Cut off the top of a pumpkin and then throw it away.

    C. Use a marker to draw the facial features.

    D. Put a candle inside the pumpkin and then light it with a lighter.

寫作能力測驗

第一部份：中譯英

說明：請將下列的一段中文翻譯成通順、達意且前後連貫的英文。

　　對很多學生而言，暑假是放鬆和玩樂的時間。對我來說卻是打工的時間。通常我會到速食餐廳找一份工作，因為我可以在這種忙碌的工作環境中學會如何服務顧客並與同事相處。這會是一個寶貴的經驗。

_____

_____

_____

_____

第二部份：英文作文

說明：請依下面所提供的文字提示寫一篇英文作文，長度約120字（8至12個句子）。作文可以是一個完整的段落，也可以分段。（評分重點包括內容、組織、文法、用字遣詞、標點符號、大小寫。）

提示：寫信給一位好友，信中包含日期、稱呼 (salutation)、結尾敬語 (complimentary close) 及簽名 (signature)。第一段描述你的近況，第二段寫目前的感想和未來的計劃。

_____

_____

_____

_____

_____

_____

_____

_____

_____

口說能力測驗

🎧 Track 40

請在 15 秒內完成並唸出下列自我介紹的句子：
My seat number is (座位號碼後 5 碼), and my registration number is (考試號碼後 5 碼).

第一部份：朗讀短文

請先利用一分鐘的時間閱讀下面的短文，然後在二分鐘內以正常的速度，清楚正確的讀出下面的短文，閱讀時請不要發出聲音。

Recent studies show that emotion may be the most important part of tipping. One study showed that there is not a strong connection between the quality of service and the size of the tip. The amount of the tip usually depends on how well the customer and the waiter interacted.

$$*\qquad\qquad *\qquad\qquad *$$

Today we use the term "Achilles' heel" to describe a weak point in someone or something that is otherwise very strong. We say this because Achilles' heel was the only weak point on his body. This shows that no matter how strong something is, even a weak point can cause trouble.

第二部份：回答問題 🎧 Track 41

共十題。題目已事先錄音，每題經由耳機播出二次，不印在試卷上。第一至五題，每題回答時間 15 秒；第六至十題，每題回答時間 30 秒。每題播出後，請立即回答。回答時，不一定要用完整的句子，但請在作答時間內盡量的表達。

下面有一張圖片及四個相關的問題，請在一分半鐘內完成作答。作答時，請直接回答，不需將題號及題目唸出。

首先請利用 30 秒的時間看圖及問題。

1. 這些人在哪裡？
2. 他們在做什麼？
3. 你認為他們很快樂嗎？是什麼讓你這麼想呢？
4. 如果尚有時間，請盡可能詳細描述這張照片。

請將下列自我介紹的句子再唸一遍：
My seat number is (座位號碼後 5 碼), and my registration number is (考試號碼後 5 碼).

跨閱英文

王信雲 編著　　車昀庭 審定

學習不限於書本上的知識，而是「**跨**」出去，學習帶得走的能力！

跨文化
呈現不同的國家或文化，進而了解及尊重多元文化。

跨世代
橫跨時間軸，經歷不同的世代，見證其發展里程碑。

跨領域
整合兩個或兩個以上領域之間的知識，拓展知識領域。

1. 以新課綱的核心素養為主軸
網羅 3 大面向——「跨文化」、「跨世代」、「跨領域」，共 24 篇文章，引發你對各項議題的好奇。包含多元文化、家庭、生涯規劃、科技、資訊、性別平等、生命、閱讀素養、戶外、環境、海洋、防災等之多項重要議題，開拓多元領域的視野！

2. 跨出一板一眼的作答舒適圈
以循序漸進的實戰演練，搭配全彩的圖像設計，引導學生跳脫形式學習，練出「混合題型」新手感，並更進一步利用「進階練習」的訓練，達到整合知識和活用英文的能力。最後搭配「延伸活動」，讓你在各式各樣的活動中 FUN 學英文！

3. 隨書附贈活動式設計解析本
自學教學兩相宜，方便你完整對照中譯，有效理解文章，並有詳細的試題解析，讓你擊破各個答題關卡，從容應試每一關！

10堂課練就TED Talks演講力

溫宥基　編著
車昀庭　審定

掌握TED Talks 演講祕訣，
上臺演講不再是一件難事。

★ 為你精心挑選的演講主題
全書共10個主題，別出心裁的主題設計，帶出不同的學習重點，並聘請專業的外籍作者編寫每一課主題的文章，讓你輕鬆融入TED Talks 演講主題。

★ 為你探討多元的關鍵議題
涵蓋豐富多元的議題教育融入課程，包括生命、資訊、人權、環境、科技、海洋、品德、性別平等之多項重要議題，讓你多方面涉獵不同領域題材。

★ 為你培養敏銳的英文聽力
每堂課的課文和單字皆由專業的外籍錄音員錄製，提升你的英文聽力真功夫。

★ 為你增強必備的實用單字
每篇課文從所搭配的TED Talks 演講影片精選出多個實用單字，強化你的單字庫。

★ 為你條列重要的演講技巧
搭配精采的10個TED Talks 演講影片，傳授最實用的演講技巧，並精準呈現演講的常用句型。

★ 為你設計即時的實戰演練
現學現做練習題，以循序漸進、由淺入深的教學引導，將每一堂課所有的演講技巧串聯並整合即完成一場英文演講，練就完美的演講力。

英文作文 這樣寫，就 OK

提升你的英文寫作能力，這一本就 OK ！

張淑娛、應惠蕙　編著／車昀庭　審定

1. 從「中英文句子基本結構的差異」、「腦力激盪」的概念談起，引導你從基礎寫作開始練習。
2. 介紹常見的英文文體，包括敘述文、描寫文、看圖寫作、說明文、書信寫作、圖表寫作與議論文，讓你充分學習每一種文體的寫作技巧。
3. 提點寫作重點與步驟，替你打下扎實的寫作基本功。
4. 補充圖表寫作的寫作技巧，符合新課綱核心素養導向，讓你先會先贏。
5. 內容豐富充實，按部就班練習，自學、教學一本就 OK ！

大考翻譯 實戰題本

王隆興　編著

1. 全新編排五大主題架構，串聯三十回三百句練習，爆量刷題練手感。
2. 融入時事及新課綱議題，取材多元豐富又生活化，命題趨勢一把抓。
3. 彙整大考熱門翻譯句型，提供建議寫法參考字詞，循序漸進好容易。
4. 解析本收錄單字補充包，有效擴增翻譯寫作用字，翻譯技能點到滿。

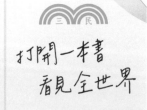

國家圖書館出版品預行編目資料

全民英檢中級模擬試題／郭慧敏編著.－－修訂三版
二刷.－－臺北市: 三民，2023
　　面；　公分

　ISBN 978-957-14-7191-4　（平裝）
　1. 英語 2. 問題集

805.1892　　　　　　　　　　　　110006689

全民英檢中級模擬試題

| 編 著 者 | 郭慧敏 |
| 內頁繪圖 | 豆 子 |

發 行 人	劉振強
出 版 者	三民書局股份有限公司
地　　址	臺北市復興北路 386 號 (復北門市)
	臺北市重慶南路一段 61 號 (重南門市)
電　　話	(02)25006600
網　　址	三民網路書店 https://www.sanmin.com.tw

出版日期	初版一刷 2010 年 6 月
	修訂三版一刷 2021 年 6 月
	修訂三版二刷 2023 年 7 月
書籍編號	S809400
I S B N	978-957-14-7191-4

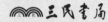